Aidan Higgins was born in Co. Kildare, Ireland, in 1927. He is the author of three previous novels, *Langrishe, Go Down* (which was filmed for BBC television with a script by Harold Pinter), *Balcony of Europe* and *Scenes from a Receding Past*. His other books include *Asylum and Other Stories* and *Images of Africa (Diary 1956–60)*. More recently he has been writing original work for radio and his highly praised *Vanishing Heroes* was the 1983 British entry for the Prix Futura. He is married with three sons and lives in London.

Aidan Higgins

BORNHOLM NIGHT-FERRY

First published in Great Britain by
Allison and Busby Ltd 1983
Published in Abacus by
Sphere Books Ltd 1985
30–32 Gray's Inn Road, London WC1X 8JL
Copyright © 1983 by Aidan Higgins

The compiler of this *Briefbuch*
wishes to thank An Chomhairle Ealaíon (Irish Arts Council)
and the American Irish Foundation for timely financial aid.
The writer of this book was assisted by a contribution from the
Author's Royalty Scheme of the Arts Council (An Chomhairle
Ealaíon), Dublin, Ireland.

This book is published with the assistance of the Arts Council (An
Chomhairle Ealaíon). Dublin, Ireland.

Printed and bound in Great Britain by
Cox & Wyman Ltd, Reading

For Nanna
who wrote the better half.

Nød laerer nøgen kvinde at spinde
Distress teaches naked women to spin
(Old Danish proverb)

Bornholm Disease. *n.* an epidemic virus infection characterized by pain round the base of the chest.

Collins English Dictionary

Love Is Blynd.

Chaucer.

I

Copenhagen, Malmö,
Ystad, Bornholm

Bornholm Diary, September 1980

Monday 8th September

It was one of those grey overcast afternoons in Copenhagen, where my true love lies. You worked until six in Thimm's empty studio across the lake. Then came, impetuous as ever, banging through the two intersecting doors and threw a thousand Kroner in ten large notes on the table. It seemed a great amount to me. Your hours, your hard-won earnings derived from the boredom of proof-reading chemical formulae or something as dry.

"Bornholm tomorrow!"

You were elated as only you can be. Alarum set for 6:00 a.m.

Tuesday 9th September

Taxi ride to the Malmö ferry through deserted city. The passengers went calmly aboard. It was hot in the saloon. We sat on a bench on the open deck under an umbrella, a thin fretting rain drizzling on the Ostsee, saw the Swedish shore. Changed Kroner in Malmö, where no bars opened until midday. We were in Sweden.

Businessmen carrying expensive briefcases occupied the red and blue station restaurant, laughed at you for inquiring when the bars opened. They sat on cushioned seats, studying documents, sipping unsugared coffee. No piped-in music disturbed their Swedish peace, their morning deliberations. It was not Paddington. All very sober in Malmö.

The train to Ystad. A tall girl never raised her eyes from a book. The jolly Malmö conductor assured us that a bus waited at Ystad dockside, but no public transport was in sight as we walked the seven hundred metres through the smell of fermentation from an unseen brewery. A long, long goodstrain was slowly emerging from what you called the stomach of a ship bound for Poland and the striking dockworkers of Gdansk.

Ystad: a place of milk-drinkers.

In the Restaurant Felix no one looked happy, the milk-drinkers murmuring in Swedish and schnapps offered by a

9

bar-lady with a sinister smile. We sat by the window. It was raining in Ystad. Slovenly Swedish soldiers in baggy green uniforms walked by Domus. Two Negroes looked out of place in the thin rain still falling. An elderly citizen bent double with *two* walking-sticks was painfully crossing the zebra lines. I was presented with an astronomic bill. We were certainly in Sweden. The schnapps had tasted of witch piss. The Bornholm ferry did not sail until six in the evening.

Lost in Ystad!

A heavy rain began to fall. We entered a dull museum. An exhibition of modern "art" revealed itself as, inter alia, a clotting of sand-castles on the floor, and some of these you kicked out of shape as you went by. A huge canvas hung on one wall. Naked soldiers were riding unsaddled horses into the surf. Adolf would have loved the musculature. We bought a bottle of wine in an empty wine-store and drank it in the embarkation hall, killing time. An outing of students were conversing together among themselves in a strange tongue, possibly Polish.

The ferry was vast as a factory; you hurried me (without a passport) by officers collecting tickets, into a glassed-in lounge a third deserted. We drank Hof beer, pulling away from Sweden. It was already dark when we reached Rönne on Bornholm. Entering the old Bar Centralcafeen I was warmly embraced by a hairy stranger who seemed to know me. We were back on Danish soil among beer-drinkers, and it felt very like Bavaria. Then the long taxi-ride in the pitch-black night to Svaneke. You said the woman driver had the Bornholm accent. Sing-song, Swedish. I recall nothing of the house. Our bedroom was under the slates. A foghorn sounded as we drifted off.

Wednesday 10th September: Svaneke

Svaneke is a Danish museum. A place for retired people, and birds. Nature is tamed into a public park, with sign-posts to indicate where you may walk. The toy house was the country seat of Thorkild Bogen, esteemed Danish author of wellwritten gloom. Books about little grey people doing little grey acts are the speciality of this kind concupiscent man. Some titles in English enlivened his library: the Letters of

Hector Berlioz. We watched aghast as an aged homosexual corpse appeared on the coloured television screen; a pencil had been driven deep into his eardrum. The accused youth seemed unburdened by guilt or regret; his defending lawyer was more sinister. It was America. The shower was boiling hot. We retired early. The Bogens had visited Belsen, where no birds would sing anymore. Helene, graduate in Eskimo studies, came from Bornholm, the Danish island facing Poland in the Ostsee. Over there in the European dark lay Zukers and Bad-Polzin, Lvov, homeland of Zbigniew Herbert, who in Berlin had attempted to tear out Coppera's hair by the roots.

In the garden stood a wooden studio, just big enough for a stove and table. Helene had sowed vegetables. We bought fresh mackerel and packets of Gauloises in the harbour shop; in the bar on the little square German tourists began to converge in a very German way on a coach. We drank Hof beer and Boonekamp, a good strong Danish schnapps.

We walked to Listed harbour, sheltering under your umbrella in a sudden shower, huddled by a low wall. You brought out a Hof from your bag. A neat harbour, neat houses. On the way back by road I saw apple trees, the Danish flag flying from tall masts in every second garden, no one about, sanatoria-style open loggias recalling *Der Zäuberberg*. The place was singularly deserted. "Russia begins at Mälmo," the Danes say sourly. What ends at Bornholm? Sedation, inner security, outer boredom, life at its nadir. The real character of the island failed to reveal itself to us. Rock.

We remained for three days and returned on the Rönne-Copenhagen night-ferry after dinner with Finn and Aase Silehoved (herringhead), your friends on Bornholm. All the berths had been booked. We dozed on green cushions amid a grim company of Germans at cards all night. A Grosz figure porcine about the jowls, a long cigarette-holder tilted at a truculent angle, voraciously read right through *Frankfurter Algemeine Zeitung*. Then a woman rose up with a hairstyle rigid as a privet-hedge. A beer-drinker was stuck fast in his chair — the Danish explorer who stayed at home. We slept as best we could. Badly.

When a greenishblue daybreak began to leak through the

ports the cardgame was still proceeding. The Elephant beer-drinker was still clamped into his chair. The heavy impassive face revealed nothing. No hand movements.

At midnight the bar had closed. There were no drunks. The night passed on the water. At half-past six in the morning the lights were turned on again and the kiosks opened. Women with toothbrushes went past to the washrooms by the campers who were laid out in rows in their sleeping-bags. It was all very orderly and quiet. That's how it was aboard the *SS Anker Kofoed*. The lounges were cleared before the calm disembarkation.

We had no trouble to find a taxi. The passengers were quietly dispersing, walking into semi-deserted Copenhagen. Then the ride through the again deserted city with you to Nørre Søgade.

Of that journey then what now remains? A meagre enough display of fruit and vegetables in the market at Ystad. The brewery smell and my torn jacket. The persistent rain, a smile lingering on Swedish lips, Sweden's folkless fields, invoking sadness; a settled land.

II

Copenhagen, Rørvig,
Bornholm, Atepmoc

CHAPTER 1: Letters 1, 2, 3 (1975)

The Sensual Memory

Letter 1

Copenhagen,
12. maj 1975

My Dearest Fitzy

I'm feeling very strange. Not good. I am ashamed to confess it. This is like the shaking period mentally, too little, too much. Accidentally words comes out. Have been working all night (in my way), will be stony tomorrow, distant.

Thanks for the pictures—grateful thanks for the picture of yourself. I've cut a little picture out from my mad youth (aged 26 years) and the picture of Marijke is $1\frac{1}{2}$ years old. Send you new ones very soon.

Flaws. I love flaws. The flaws make the person. The defects are the heart of the matter. The virtues we have in common.

I send you some writing-material, too—all handstolen. Thanks in forward for books and other words. I'm not up in German, unfortunately. Have already red your first novel. It was a very depressing book, I must say. If that's your Ireland, I do understand you left. Standstill, deadly boredom, impenetrable selfishness, bog, all the worst in myself.

Your plans for next summer,—a new side of you—a side I didn't know, a side I didn't expect, a side I feel home at, a making dreams side. In most other directions you are a stranger to me. I wasn't right the very first evening. You was all excitement, no homefeeling. I am so glad that you are glad. You couldn't give me a more delicate love-present. I could *maybe* come again this summer, for 1 or 2 weeks.

Now—important: Opposite to you (?) I believe in the Big Subjectivity. It's so tempting to be unhappy. I am ashame. But I miss the love. Our curious long Cataluña kiss, changing in strength and tone during the same kiss, lingering, nearly soporific and—by a turn of the tongue or only the thought …

Curious kiss, so musical.

This week has been very long, filled with thoughts, thoughts, thoughts. Too much. I've been writing to you all week, now I'm writing again, could go on for hours, like our kissing. *Brüderlein, ich bin ja dein, nicht war? Es ist wahr. Ist es wirklich wahr?*

The spring, the steady, warm spring has arrived in Copenhagen.

Elin.

Letter 2

Copenhagen
16. maj 1975

My beloved Fitzy—

At last: *Das Leben ist wieder wunderbar, eine wunderbar Tannenbaum.* The sun is shining, 3 days-off at Rørvig are before me, I am not pregnant. Got the answer today. Have been sick by the thought to be pregnant not daring to bear the child, fearing (knowing) that (my) magic wasn't enough to the everyday. Sick by the thought to remove the child from the Grassy-Place.

Now "God" made the decision, I'm breathing again, look optimistical—broadly—at our possibilities. We are not old tomorrow. This in a hurry in order to let you know, that I'm glad again, have had a very bad time, missing you, doubting you. Haven't told you directly about it, but surely you have felt it.

Concerning: feeling home.

It wasn't incorrect, what I said, about feeling incomplete. You was the forgotten world, the déjâ-vu, you hardly recognize, you touched deep level in me. Only seldom was I "myself" in your company, and when, you refused it. It hurted me sometimes, you perceived me so absolutely physical, but in the same time you and Spain, gave all kinds of *Gestalt* a forgotten value. Therefore the excitement, as, when you in a dream, are a hairbreath from the answer. Will the dream continue, until you understand its message? When I said:—You make me feel home—I ment it in a superficial way, something with milieu, but it was something else, much deeper, almost not true any longer, almost forgotten. Not forgotten in words but in action. The sensual memory of you is going to disappear, replaced by reflections. I need your good influence. Now—what did you see in me (not in the coquettish meaning) but *what*—what landscapes—did you see?

Send also the other epistle, so you can know me. I'm very much up and down, or simply a little stupid, as I've often told.

I'm reading your short stories for the moment. They make a much greater impression to me than the novel. They make, in fact, a great impression, remind me of that mood, I slight felt (behind your talking-word of which I only understood a quarter) when you told your long, cruel, tender bedstories.

Ich liebe dich – or I love the idea of you – cannot find out – but you are lying as a strength in me.

Ever yours,
Elin.

PS: I've seen very much at your picture. All the time there was something which disturbed me, something I didn't recognized. That's the feature round your mouth. Your mouth has changed. On the picture you see a man captured of hesitations, a person full of intentions, nearly treachery—a bit of an imposter, a person for whom an action first is a crime in that moment it is brought to the light. A person you can deal in. Like that I never saw you. Always I saw your cheerfulness. Chinese cheerfulness.

(Unsigned)

Letter 3

København
27. maj 1975

My beloved Fitzy—
Got your beautifull letter this morning because I went late from home today. Please, my dear, send letters to Denmarks Radio-adres, here I'll get them in the morning and my day will not be determined of hope for letter, waiting at home,

alone at the top of the steps for hours. I red your letter while I had breakfast at the sunny terasso at DR and understood all of it at once, but red it over again. It was exiting in an odd way to sit there among people, occupied by "the occurences of the world", reading your letter. Like being at dinner-party, touching the sex of your beloved under the tablecloth. Exiting and painfull. Lighted a cigaret and look normal. Now I've looked up all the words I provable not "can". Most in order to continue the occupation.

Just today I was photographed for leigitimationcard. Asked the photo-chap to make an extra copy. Was conscious thinking of you under the shooting. You write: "You are the strongest representative of a *type* I cannot resist." It is not an unelegant way to put it. If you think so, then it is *really* true. And the papercutting is a selected illustration. I want everything of your writings, from the past and from the future. You will make me very happy if you send me something. Also tell me what you are writing now (if you use to do so to anybody. If you like it.) Please, repeat the plot. I never really understood it at Atepmoc, just enough to couldn't forget. Very often there I was going to ask you for the drawing, the selfportrait. Exactly that drawing I want very much. I could make photostat from the book and send the book back again? Want the other too (8—eight—years???). Then maybe you could select some pieces to read first, it's a enormous work to me, to read complicated english. But not your letters. Your letters I understand immedeately (and then I confirm my understanding by the dictionary).

I think I understand the term "finished". And its result: "Beginning". Miss you very much, still still. In a way more. Not so desperate but deeper. And steady. Don't you understand it was with sorrow I wrote, that I was going to loose the sensual memory of you? It was. I know very well that the rest is "figments of the imagination", monologues.

Last weekend I tried to make an outline of the days with you, very short and only about what we did. The *Praha*-story failed, now it will takes at least 4 weeks before it will be brought in paper, but it is not a serious thing, not a serious written story. Written to a newspaper and written before I met you … Send it anyway when it comes. Send the first story now instead. Not because I like to do it but because anything is better than cowardice.

Does it embarrass you that I try to write, my love? I feel it does, that you are afraid I mis-use something which may have been more beautifull by not being expressed. What can I do? The words are at me, you are not. We didn't made love enough, far from enough, much too little. My dear. And you know it. "*Dine kys glemmer jeg ikke.*"

So curious to see that line in your letter in my language. Like a prophecy you don't understand untill it has come true. It is rare a lie turns into a beautifull truth. I saw the line immedeately, the want for you went as a cut through me, again it was intolerable not to be with you. When can I give you a new kiss?

29, maj 1975

I want to send this letter together with a picture of myself. I'm expecting the DR-legitimation-photo and some others with Marijke and I from the 40 years-birthday of Steffen. Feel that you want a picture rather much, can "tell more than many words." I got your amulet back today, framed in silver. It will be around my neck from now, remind me of happiness, of the time of shaking. (I happen to write about love no matter what subject I find.) The wood interior is not my home. I send you picture from my home one day.

Looking forward for the bottle of 103. And hearing news about you. Marijke is squint. Rørvig is the summer place. I was sitting at the inn Withsun-Sunday having Boonekamp, had just read *Torn og Engel* (again or for the first time I don't remember), was writing something about it for you. Marijke was running around (I recognize her footsteps through the traffic-noise, I'm anyway a true mother), until she discovered me writing. Then she wanted the pencil, want to make drawings. I told her to wait, she asked how long. I said: Very long. After some minutes she invented a new technique: painting with smashed green leaves and all color flowers. Selfish mothers creates gifted children.

Did your son come at Withsun-time? Do you see Pastor and Pernille frequently? Are you sometimes talking about me? When do you get up in the morning? What do you eat? Is it

19

dark in the evening and how warm are the days? Here in Denmark it is very cold, blowing, raining. Is Mr Larry Rivers back? Is Hannel coming this summer? Are you playing chess alone? Are you sunburned? Do you ever go for walks alone? Have you got a chimney-hat?

I have imagined my second-coming to Atepmoc un-count times. I should be more beautiful than you ever saw me before, slight sunburned, my hair a little longer, dressed in a white linen-dress. We would go to Hotel Cataluña, let the-man-in-the-lift take us direct up to our room. Then we lock the door and stay wordless on the floor and you kiss me while I stay up the wall and you open my dress while we are kissing each other and I open your cloth and put my hands under your shirt and you will go up in me immediately and you will come in me nearly just then.

Did you love me much the day at the Third River? Really? That day was to me the turn from a loveaffair to love. *Das Bad an sich. Das Knepp an sich.*

31. maj

"My Self" or "Not My Self" as the princess said. You act like you don't understand me when I write: Only selden I was "myself" together with you. You scold me, you persuade me (oh so beautifull beautifull) to realize, that "I was never more myself than when I was with you". Of course you are right, my dear. Of course. *Because* you went so deep, there was nearly nothing left from many years' depositing, many years' habit, style, manners, all that I called "myself", to put in this "   " in order to make you understand.

Indeed you got me naked.

But just like it was hard to believe that I was beautifull without cloth—and I was catched by modesty when you unexpected came to the terrace—just like that, it was very difficult to me to believe, that I was meaningfull without language, that I was beautifull without cloth. I felt lost, insufficient, I needed the language both to protect and express my happiness. I needed the language to make hymns to your honour, my love, you who showed me the beauty in the wordless world.

Yes, most of all I needed the words to tell you about that. I love the language, my own and others, the language as tool, the language which is keeping or effacing, the language you can come to the truth with or be lying with. I needed the words to entertain you, to amuse you, to put my seal into your heart so you can never forget me.

At last you got me nearly convinced that I was good enough without words, that I was beautifull enough without cloth. The very last time in Cataluña (after the "sacrificial *Kuss*") I went out of bed, quite naked, and washed my pussy with a corner of the towel and you observed me from the bed. I smiled at you through the mirror and for the first time I was sure that I was beautifull, that I—while in a accidental hotelroom with a corner of a starched linentowel washed my sex—did something beautifull.

Am longing for you. I think I mean: I need you because there is no "*Sehnsucht*" in my longing. I am longing for you rather like a cure than a person—yes, also a person, but a dumb person.

How can I go without you? How can you go without me? How can you possibly send me a letter without starting: When can you come back to Atepmoc? Why only maybe? For how long time? How can you avoid to respond, direct, that line? There can be many reasons: sweet Hannel, wife, sons, working-peace disturbed, trouble in Atepmoc, not to disturb a successful loveaffair (in fake German) …

Then I've looked at it from the other side: As a fineness from you. Any direct reason, any name, would be raw. And a little wrong. I've choosed the last version. And realized your wisdom. You are surely right Fitz. You were so often right in Atepmoc, my love. I could say nothing to you now because of the distance in body and mind. You are another person. Everything are monologues. We don't know each other, no. We exited to a high degree each others' dreams. We don't know each other, we are dreaming. Everything depends on if we are clever enough to dream. And believe in our dreams. And realize our dreams so fervently we are able to. That was what I meant by magic. What did you mean?

Love from Elin

CHAPTER 2: Letters 4, 5, 6, 7

The Pools of Rio Juan Rojo

Letter 4

Goatshed
Atepmoc
España
6 May 75

Dearest Elin,

You left your Cross behind, hung on a nail by the fireplace. What shall I do with it? I returned yesterday. Had a surprisingly good time after your departure. In Malaga it was a day for the subnormales. I found boots for Marijke, little pet, green clogs for 550 pesetas, if you give me her size. Did she like our presents: the little hand-mirror, the big bone-comb? Was Steffen (who takes photos of you for me) pleased to have you back? Were you, more important, pleased to be back with him?

Found an old snail eaters' place in the Brothel Quarter, drank beer with a Fräulein and her dull Canadian boyfriend, drank gins alone, got back to Hotel Cataluña late, was given a fine room, our door (Numero 33) was open when I passed, our beds made up, you were not there. You had gone to work on old Islands Brygge next morning when I was having coffee and churros at the counter of Café Español, you were not sitting by the window, taking a morning beer. On Sunday every place where we had been was closed. I walked for hours. It wasn't too bad without you as I had feared. The happiness you had given me, first offered me, continued, even without you, *Schwesterlein*.

The bus journey back was good, too. I spoke to the grave-digger. In Dolores' Bar got into conversation with a man from the hills, on Women's so-called Liberation, very deep stuff. Nils Bud's nice wife was cooking something good behind bead-curtain, glancing guardedly around. She disapproves of my morals, or lack of them, referring several times to Sexual Emancipation (that bogey), I could not follow to whose she was referring. Bud the Botanist glided silently in and out, with that look of fixed amaze stamped on his features—a tree stuck by lightning—coming and going, as is his wont; the skinflint! I pointed to the end of the bar, conspicuously deserted, and spoke warmly of you. The Buds looked askance with compressed lips.

Today it poured with rain after thunder that came right down the kitchen chimney with a bellow of demons. It clears. Behold our clean sheets fly from the roof like sails!

I miss your morning Coffee-*Kuss* and even your deep disturbing *Nacht-Kuss* (with eyes closed, as if tasting the bitterest bitterness and the sweetest sweetness together), see your greenish lynx-eyes watching me in the cracked mirror when I shave me. I miss you stalking around naked and I miss you naked in bed. I regret that the fire was never lit. We lit our own fires. I write to you youngly, for you have made me feel young again, although I never felt old. Curious ambit, disinterested adviser. Young you made me. Your touch was strange. Your approach stranger. We began very fast and kept it up. What did we do on Tuesday and Wednesday of last week? My diary is blank, and I forget.

If you sleep with anybody you must tell me. Chance favours the prepared mind.

I write to you, my dearest *Schwesterlein*, in order to get the habit. Favour your *Brüderlein* with a prompt reply, *por favor*. And I send you all my love, dearest one.

Ihne Brüderlein

PS: Please send map of Copenhagen. And write soon. Love you.

Letter 5

Dearest Elin,

Have been working from time I rise, trying (without much success) not to think of you in my bed, until 2:00 am this week. Some sort of story may be emerging. I write very few of them, thought they were all lost in oblivion.

On way to Correos today encountered J'Espoir who told me that bitch B. was departing tomorrow. Will ask her to kindly take bottle of 103 to you with your Cross, which you may be missing. Also a little note. Pleased to receive your letter. Glad to hear you are missing me in the body, as I you, but more so. I did not invent your beauty, *Schwesterlein*, you have it. Sight of you naked so soon sliding into Roman bath or rock-pools of Rio Juan Rojo, was something to see.

Or coming up the ramp for the first time to stout Luis' bar, when you put the odd question: Did I find you masculine. Your shyness came as a surprise, a true modesty. I miss our bogus Deutsch, drinking your coffee, I miss that. You write that you had only started on the magic. Me too.

Took your letter to Aurelio's bar, had a Lomo and two coffees. Not eating much, working 15 hours without fatigue, but with great excitement, smoking too much. I suppose the excitement and tirelessness is the residue of you in me, because there is also happiness in it, which rarely happens with me, as there is always something (in the other) against it. We didn't even know each other long enough to find flaws.

Have washed all the sheets. The inquisitive neighbours must wonder what's hidden behind all that bedlinen. I take them down and there is nothing.

I write this in a hurry. Will give your colleague that cognac, that Cross. It conveys to you a little of my love. *Schwesterlein*.

Your Fitzy

Goatshed,
Atepmoc,
España
23 May 75

My Dearest Elin,

Sunday 18th you were a fortnight gone and it seemed an Eternity. Sorry I missed the last sight of you crossing the apron after the worried Liverpool bunch, but by then I had retired into Servicio to count my pesetas. Walked out feeling peculiar as you might have guessed and found bus stop near the Other Airport, spoke to man of the soil, smoked, saw your flight (I suppose it was) depart, ascending in almost angry fashion and aimed straight for Denmark, pulling a part of me after it. And that was long ago. And I am missing you since.

Glad you did not conceive in the Grassy-Place. I loved you so much that day, with your Red Indian headband and bleeding feet, bathing (naked so fast) and then eating (eating so slow), and telling me about churches plundered by damned rapacious Vikings, your blood in them, I wanted to give you something of me.

Please miss me and don't "doubt" me.

I never had a bad time with you, all your moods delighted me, even the bad ones. How can you possibly say that you were not yourself? Who are you then? You were never more yourself than when you were with me. Forgive me if I yarned away too long at stories—my past really it was I wished to show you—even if you didn't understand all of it, no matter. You are not stupida. Though you seem to think you are, like the curious notion (not mine) of your un-femininity. I have rarely met a lady more feminine, less masculine, than you. I remember you waiting below, knocking on the 90-year-old old woman's door, she deaf as a post, you looking up, coming up. It was the Shaking-Time, I was shaking with happiness.

May have to go to Ireland in October. Could you perhaps come for a week or a fortnight then? It would not be as the walk back from Canillas de Albaida in the evening, the fellows and their girls linking arms on the road, someone playing a guitar on the threshing circle, but it would be something like it. October and May are the best months in that odd country.

But I hardly dare to think of you walking with me in Dublin.

Dine kys glemmer jeg ikke.

(Unsigned)

Letter 7

My dearest Elin,

Hit hit hit how strange even in your poor English which I love that you hit at me your parenthesis are extraordinary I felt the wood inebia (???) was not your room I did not feel it your home I would know your home more parenthesis that child squinting that background wood something on the wall I tried to feel you there I could not feel you there you were not there I wanted you to be there

out of the middle of your pages images strike at me it's your feelings striking at me there are no other feelings for me they were hitting at me hitting at me once again how extraordinary, once again

how can I start a letter like that??? when every morning I wake up missing you every morning missing you and you fading away the sensual memory fading away how can I even live if the sensual memory is fading away if bits and pieces of you are fading away how much I desire your happiness you at home (where is that??) waiting at the top of the steps for hours you in Rørvig sitting in the inn (why traffic noise?) and Marijke asking for a pencil many times I feel you there a place I cannot see and you walking around because of that I am lost you walking in places I cannot imagine I want you always to be in places I cannot imagine where I can catch hold of you how strange you cannot feel yourself as beautiful, your eye in the mirror, you naked, I felt something had happened to you before, you could not see yourself, believe yourself, the beautiful naked woman, how much I wanted you to come to details in your letters, say how it was with us, no we did not make love enough, walked out the other morning at 7:30 am with Larry and passed our Rocky Place and a Piney Place and another Higher Rocky Place where you were almost naked how much I regretted not having made love to you there the last chance the only hope high up in the evening the sun behind the clouds the clouds hiding the mountains and you there and I in what a state what a turmoil afraid to look at you making love hardly enough to say me to express me to catch hold of you to die in you because of longing, no we did not make love enough I dying in your voice never touching a woman before never wanting before never loving before that was you

went to bed with another tried to invent you it was all trying to invent you trying to kiss again it didn't work it would never work it was idiotic, please do not say if you go to bed with another I do not want to hear that, it would be as poor for you as for me, I was trying to memorize you again it doesn't work forgive me if I write in this way I would prefer to howl or groan because when I try to think of you here I am lost in bits and pieces, no touch no hearing no night no day no food no nothing you are somewhere else my life is somewhere else the others have disappeared, all the others there are no others no touch no Cataluña kiss nor Grassy Place no nights here no you asleep in the next room no candle gutting no water in the bathroom no shower no Third River no restaurant on the Malaga seafront no face of you that I already have forgotten right about a photo I miss your face I want to see your face I wake up and try to invent you naked with me but it's only myself and I am nothing without you I miss you very much

this kind of letter is idiotic what other way can I put it the details of you kissing each other and putting your hands and go up in you and come in you how hard that is to hear if you are so far away, bits and pieces of the old loves all shattered

27

and there is only you the colours you wear the way you walk what clothes you are to wear like asking me do I want to live again am I serious about wanting to live again in this way, we are at a dinner party fucking each other under the table, light a cigarette and look normal, exactly that was what your eyes told me, it will never be normal again, we don't know each other, you say, we know each other, all the rest is absurd, there is only the time in Luis Gordo's bar when you came in through the door, there is only the time when we talked for the first time below the bakery, there is only the time when I kissed you for the first time, there is only what happened after, nothing else means anything, you walking naked in the bedroom I was afraid to watch, you asleep I was afraid to touch, you in your half-awake mornings I was afraid to trouble, you horizontal or vertical such a dream, is that it, no dream but all the wanted things one ever wanted in one thing, person, in you, live in your hair in your mouth give you nothing, why should you need food when you have me, live on carrots, live on old dreams that are now seen as rotten and come true

no beer no candles no welcome no bed no night no breath no Elin walking around saying this food is ill-cooked we have nothing left but rotten carrots we have nothing left except ourselves we don't exist no mouth to speak no eyes to see no hair to give out its scent no clothes to be removed no bad temper no bad words no boots to be thrown into another room

I overlooked the back of one page yes Larry is back no Hannee is not coming this summer no I am not playing chess alone yes I am sun burned no I do not go for walks alone but with Larry yes I have the chimney pot hat, my days that are my days, I am working on the novel, you say love at the Third River, it happened almost immediately for me, with the shaking.

Knepp what the hell is *Knepp*, I miss your pseudo-Deutsch, mein *Schwesterlein* write soon I miss you I miss you
  (Unsigned)

CHAPTER 3: Letters 8, 9

Dichtung und Wahrheit

Letter 8

Copenhagen
14. juni 75

My dear Fitzy

I can come to you when you want it and where, will always be able to get hold of money for a ticket to Atepmoc or Dublin or Potsdam.

I am tired, no worn out from the suffering of the miss of you. Enough, enough. I must go to new thought-courses about you, I'm exhausted of this longing for living together with you, I'm far-off to Marijke, I'm not able to write anything but letters for you, think other beings are indifferent, flat. I'll stop this flood of *Dichtung und Wahrheit* around our lovestory, stop it, stop it, I want to live with you or make it to a story, to a parable in my heart, not trying the one and hoping the other. I'm too greedy, too violent, that's why things never are delicious and easy to me, other women have holiday-affair, nurse it for a while and then forget it natural way. A lovely vacation that year.

Often I feel that our love is invented (well, love is), that we outbet each other in our letters—"look how much I love you," all this words make a meeting-again difficult, risky, maybe impossible. Murder. I prefer this risk. I will come to you when you say so. And let the love die or myself die.

I will come to you when you say so.

This letter will be the last despair letter.

No, I will not tell you if I go to bed with others.

Yes, I have a mistrustfull heart, I was born mistrustfull to myself, only you make me forgetting it. How long? Yes, something wrong happened to me once, many little things, the same as happen to everybody, I remember that and not something else. Everything "happens" to everbody, a invariable flair keeps us to something, the rest are forgotten. I give you a accidental picture: My first school-ball.

I had a dress, thin, thin wool, faint blue with grey in-weaved spots (down, really), heart-shape cut, tight waist, width from hips. That dress should compensate an endless, diffuse, unreal childhood: When I am 8- 9- 10- 11- 12- 13 years old everything will change.

Immediately I came to the "gaily decorated gymnasium" I knew the dress was wrong. And the dress was me, you must remember, my code. The other girls shined as colorrich gallinaceous birds, circulated round, cackling. They were on the right place.

The boys squeezed themselves, red in comb, exited and ashamed, not yet quite in the right place. The dancing began, I sat on a bench (they were narrow) for a couple of hours. It's not so painfull, you just let the state continue, do not touch it, are quiet. Then a boy came, asked for a dance. He was much shorter than me, kept the hand tied up on my back, because it was sweaty I suppose. By an absolute effort, a burning wich, I succeeded to transform the minutes on the floor into what they showed: A boy dancing with a girl.
—Everything has changed.—

Then a girl came (one of those who choosed an incarnation as tormentor).—Well, you was dancing with Sven?
—Yes, I said, yes I did.

She smiled and said very fast:—Well, it was because I gave him sixpence in order to do it.

I was *ugly*. So ugly that every day three girls beat me. They waited after school and then they beat me, because I was so ugly. I bit my nails and stammered. I masturbated. And for all that they beat me. *Beat* me! I was dung of the earth I tell you and deserved to be beaten. So naturally I grew uglier and uglier. Then I would end up in a tree masturbating and tormented by the whole world. And every day school again and the three tormentors waiting. My life was misery then, a deep deep misery. I go to dinnerparty at Bogens' in one hour, one of his friends pick me up, the chap who has translated the I CHING into danish, Thorkild the Cunt Thief says we fits each other, are you suffering now? you make me very much suffering, I want revenge, I want no reasons for revenge, I know the chap is dry, I miss you. I fear you. I fear there is

30

nothing to fear. We ought to have some years together called "On Exploring". Yes.

Elin

PS: The Map: nearly in the middle of Copenhagen you find 4 blue quadrangles. This are called the Lakes. In one of the two middle lakes you find a (1), written with a red pencil. That my home.

PPS: I will try—really try—to be calm, no more sad letters send in a hurry. I will write to you frequently and normally.

Letter 9

17. juni 1975

My dearest Fitzy
I sent you a hard and desperate letter yesterday by normal mail, I hope this will arrived first.

I think I've told you about the old chinese oracle-book I CHING, which means *the book of the changes*. About you and me I had not asked. Untill yesterday after sending the bad letter, after that minute I felt something were wrong. Therefore I asked I CHING this evening. I send you the answer. I feel so happy. Time doesn't matter. We have lots of time, do not dispair we will be saved. The answers are much longer but it is hard to translate and you don't need many words or fat food, you are sharp and creating yourself. Self-strengthening.

Talk with Larry Rivers about the Hexagrams if you want to hear again how blessed we are. Forgive me my doubting.

Ever yours
Elin

PS: Knepp means fuck, *the fuck*. You know, Kant has this wellknown idea: *Das Ding an sich* = the thing-in-itself, the reality as it is apart from our judgement. Well.

31

Question: Will a meeting again between Fitz and Elin be filled with love?

Answer: Hexagram 14

Name: Possession of the Great

Sign: The Flame and the Sun (the fire is shining widely and brings everything into light)

The judgement: Possession of the great brings elevated happiness.

The Line: That person, whose truth is accessible but nevertheless is worthy, finds happiness.

This hexagram is changing into

Hexagram 1

Name: The Creative, The Heaven

Sign: The Sun and the Sun (the primitive force is light-giving, strong, witty)

The judgement: The Creative brings elevated happiness promoted through perseverence.

NB. The words are direct translated, not mine.

Resumé:

16. april, 11:30—at Pepinos place at the Plaza.
We said hello and nothing more to each other for the next couple of hours.
When the bar closed I said: Immedeately I saw you …
—Really, you said, lifted the eye-brow and asked if I wanted to see your house.
We sat on your bed and you told me about the Habsburg's sad and obvious end and twined the scarf around my neck and kissed me.

17. april, 3 o'clock
I sat at Espejo, you at Luis. I crossed the Plaza slowly in order to make you discovering me. Suddenly I saw you in the door and lifted the hand as I had expected you there.
We drank gin. I talked much. I shaked and must sit down.
The odd question.
Suzanne and Pernille and little Anna came. I went.
10 o'clock I nocked on the wrong door. You heard me and saved us for the second time in our short life.
We slept late and waked up early.

18. april—this day I only dare to give titles:
The Third River. The Bath. The Grassy-place.
The home-coming: The sky, my falls, the Turner-light over the houses in the outskirts of Atepmoc, Coffee, Tappas with little strong fishes at Aurelios.
I wanted to sleep at my self that night. You followed me home.
Gin at Dolores very late, I told you about Steffen.
… "for a while." My feeds was bleeding.

19. april
Came to your house 3 o'clock.
We was shaking like mads. Drank the Champagne of the Pastor, made Florencio to an Italian. You gave me amulets and a flowering cherry-branch. You did.
Nerja. We could eat nothing of Jesú's good food. Awfull evening. I was unhappy, unsure, said cruel things instead of loving you. Turned the backs to each other and slept.

33

20. april, sunday.
Stayed in bed all the day. Your long bed-stories that day.
—I'm starving, I complained.
—Take a rotten carrot you bitch, you answered and we laughed, many times, every time.
I learned the struck of the church bell and the little window across your bed to the bottom that day, my skinn opened that day.
But CHILE were closed. Lomo at Luis instead. I told you about my every-day and about what is on my walls. Melancholy. I felt boring. When did we invent the kitchen-german?
Already here?

21. april
Went to Malaga with Suzanne, Jesper, Sue Campion and Tobin.
Got a snake in the bag. Bought wrong shoes. A wasted day, now it ... necessary to move up, and stay with you.

22. april
I catched my things at Suzanne and Jesper, didn't used a suitcase but Nils discovered me anyway.—Well, you are leaving us now, he asked.
—No, only for a while (a usefull word), I said.
I put the peg on the wall with my shoeheel, hang the cross at the fireplace, boiled vegetables and stood for the first time at the door with the fly-net and looked upon you in your writing-room.

23. april. wednesday.
The unbath child.
You worked a couple of hours in the afternoon. We started eating again (*Coq au vin*). In the evening we went almost to Gloria Lunn's house.

24. april
Hairwash. Bit tips. I weared the northafrican home-coat.
Mountain-walk in the afternoon. It was very hot. You sat on a stone I lay on my knees and kissed your sex (prick??).

—We make a beautifull picture now, I said.
—As please God, you said.
We missed the Pines.
Gin at Pernille and Pastor at the street outside thier house.
Chess in the evening for the first time. I win and don't believe my own eyes, you neither.

25. april, friday.
The Pastor thundered on the door one o'clock, we was still in bed. Dinner at the Pastor and his wife. You became very drunken, quarrel about who had the right, the first-right to Atepmoc: Larry Rivers, you or they. Then about nightly meetings at highways.
—Only she understands me, you said and pointed threatening at me. We went home, you stopped incesant. We went up to your writing-room and I got on the floor between your legs and cried. You looked at me, didn't cry.

26. april, saturday.
The walk to the closed electricity-house. Was you equally surprise as I, that the door was open? Fits so well to the fairytale.
Santa Anna, Canillas, the doors. The girls and the boys dancing and singing. I was so happy. Also then I was happy.
Gin at Dolores with Suzanne and Jesper. Lomo at Luis. (You bought a plug which didn't fit, I white yarn I didn't use).

27. april, sunday.
Stayed in bed all the day, half-starving. Aurelio's place, coffee, cognac, tappas and fish. You pointed out people for me, told about them. The rain came. Early home, played chess, third time you took my Queen.

28. april
Rain. Chicken-soup which tasted like hell. You was very talkactive that day, stayed in the kitchen. Don't remember the evening, maybe I went down to Suzanne's house 11 o'clock, missed her, met her at the Plaza 12 o'clock? I think so. You stayed at the kitchen-window when I went. You was reading when I came home. I was happy to be home again.

35

29, april

Rain. Pernille and Anna came, P. lent a book, put in the fireplace ... I went for a walk around the town, couldn't really find home, understood the direction but was on the wrong level all the time.

Chicken-soup, by Jove, once more. Chess. Jesper Høeck in the night, talking.

30. april.

Your dream about carrying me secretly on your back. The verandah-day. You gave me Michaux. Oil, sun, love, All entrances seemed possible.

Lomo at Espejo in the evening. Rafael drank with us.

We played chess and eated at first floor. I needed my language that evening.

1. may.

We washed cloth.

The shops closed surprising at 2 o'clock. I bought food in a hurry (at Mercedes) met Pernille, went home with her for an hour, having bad conscience, you starving. I went to your writing-room, you showed me what you had written and said: Without language—no thoughts. I knew it was true. It almost broke my heart, amputated our connection. I understood it too concrete.

2. may

Still delightfull weather. I was paralysed by dispair in the morning, wouldn't get up, you went out and bought food. We went to the verandah again, made that deal, that you should work for some hours and then we would go for a walk in the mountains. We did neither, ment we had hurts in our legs. Don't remember the evening.

3 may, saturday.

Packing. Lunch at Suzanne at 12 o'clock. I asked you for money. Leave at Espejo at 3 o'clock. The busjourney to Malaga. Cataluña bang at the Cathedral. Presents for Marijke. Malaga-wine and miniature-seamonster. The lovely dinner. The Buñuel-bar at the Harbour ("in the depths of the sea …") Dispair and drunkenness prevents love.

4. may, sunday.
Exhaustion. I kissed you and knew it was the last time.
The failing breakfast, the dread of the time, the hunting of the watches,—for the first time I saw you deeply nervous. The wrong airport, the first leave, heavy as mire. Your re-coming, your watch was an hour before. Gin at the airbuilding-terasso. I went to the toilet, my bunch had disappeared, confused, light leave. I may remind of Coppera.

I looked for you in the windows, you wasn't there.

I was calm in the plain, red something which nearly interested me. Then the pain came for the first time. The thought seeks a way out, beat the head against the wall as a fool in his cell: "You are here, not there."

CHAPTER 4: Letters 10, 11, 12

"In the Depths of the Sea"

Letter 10

Atepmoc—
20/6-75

I knew you were violent, felt your love would be difficult, terrible. And now I have it, you have given it to me, and I take it, and it is terrible. And I can't stop writing to you in this way, and I can't stop missing you. And please do not confess about a dry man who "fits" you; I am so jealous of you, feel so possessive about you, that Knud Anderson incident and even an innocent-looking tube of vaginal jelly makes me jealous.

I try and imagine you and Marijke there, and I feel like smiling, the picture is so agreeable, you and her there. The idea of you being a mother, and such a loving, strange mother, charms me. Don't you know you have finished the others for me, didn't you know that? I mean sweet Hannel (as you call her) and Hannelore-over-Havel. Both suddenly vanished the time you strolled onto the plaza, when I first kissed you on my bed and you opened your eye, I knew I had been longing for you for a long time, and there you were. Everything you did had a rightness and also a mystery about it, beginning with your voice and what you said, and then without clothes, so it's exactly in order that you should move the red table up to the window and I go out from the Goatshed and you are not there, but off drinking gin with the Pastor, and then you go out again and get "lost," that's exactly correct too, because, such is my feeling for you, that you are forever getting lost and coming back, just to make it a little sour and then sweet again

I like your diary of our time here, that's okay too. I like your dream of a hotel room and the door locked and we slowly beginning to torture each other with caresses. I am glad to hear that you miss me, because it would be awful to come to you, panting from a long distance, and receive a cool reception. I miss you too, every morning I wake up and want to have you There are not even rotten carrots here now. I love the way you write that *Brüderlein* is gone and there remains only my name, my pompous name that I never believed in until you spoke it. For me too sweet *Schwesterlein* has vanished. It was part of the merry time we had with each other, so quickly over, these two ghosts, brother and sister ghost from an invented Germany, much better than the real one.

I have found with great difficulty where you live, the pencil mark is so exact I couldn't see it. The lakes look like a river, even with bridges over them, a blue green place between cemeteries and parks, so that's where you hang out. What's that Fug ... the thing in Sortedams 50? Do you walk in Holmens Kirkegaard? I never knew that philosopher's name was the same as a graveyard. What's Slot (palace)? What's Have (Rosenborg's)? Do you cycle always the same way, or different ways, passing those grand palaces, no doubt exciting dry men in cars. Dry bitch, I give you big tip, I put him into you every possible way I can, so you want nothing but me, nothing else can hope to satisfy you, all those bits and pieces flying around, or just left there, almost forgotten, and with one blow all together, strange, strange to put my arms around you and feel the shaking. You never looked so beautiful as when we drank gin that day in Café Español, I was sitting there but I was racing, running rings around you, being with you made me so happy, recovering from that kiss.

Everything went right that day in a manner that seldom happens with me. With the two H's many times all went wrong; they were real loves but I suspect wrong for each time, whereas our times and needs are ideally matched. At all events I have never moved so fast (for me) or been so certain. It's almost comical, if it wasn't so deadly serious. Suddenly you were there in your underclothes, your head lost in old stuff hanging above you, suddenly I was sleeping with you, suddenly I was dreaming about you, you had calmly stepped into my dreams in your underclothes. You were hanging around my neck before the reception desk of a strange hotel, situated in some country (Greece?) where I have never been (but it looked rather Dutch, a low place).

I look at your page 1 and see "greedy and violent," your

notion of that being "Elin," and am amused. You, that, ha! I love very much your downright way of saying you will come to me when I say so. The longing is not "wrong placed," because I have it for you too. The school dance is very much your humour. Gallinaceous?? Boys are brutes; little girls are bitches.

Please write me a letter describing your day, or weekends, or Rørvig. Does your flat face towards these lakes. I cannot imagine you in that eerie night you have up there in June. An Australian painter named Dupree has been painting Paco here. I play chess, am told my game improves but I cannot feel it. A chap who used to sleep with my wife has come here to do battle with Ludwig Wittgenstein, of all people; his arch-enemy. He laughs all the time and calls everybody "Che." Once I was very jealous of him. He has a kind heart, whereas I haven't, except for very exceptional cases. My family arrive next Tuesday at 7:a.m. I have not seen them for seven months.

I found in the bed 2 hair slides of yours and 2 toffees. I cannot see your face. I half-see your long back, that disturbs me so much, although delights me would be more to the mark. Making love to you on the terrace in the sun and in the oil was like flying in the clouds, the famous Centaur. You know that legend about men and women? The two parts are trying to join, one part galloping around the world disguised as a horse. When I love you that way I feel joined to you in a manner that will not allow you escape. When you say we didn't love enough, make love enough, it pains me a little. The failures at the beginning, almost willed by you, were a way of slowing up, and we needed to slow up. The Cataluña Kuss clinched matters. We have found each other for sure. The dancing began. I was making up for that "gaily decorated gymnasium" (I almost wrote "Museum"). I'll make up for everything that went wrong for you, my dearest.

I couldn't make out your odd reference (journal) to "in the depths of the sea," but days later remembered it. I liked very much that place, those hours, that beer, your eyes, then the wine, not-permitted-wine that was ours, that lovely room, the non-dark. I remember waking for a minute and you were climbing into your single bed, and then I went to sleep. Those mornings with you, either in bed or in the next room, were for me a most happy time, full of happiness. In three or four hours I go to a dinnerparty at La Lunn's cortijo. Party of five. Something good is being cooked up and Dupree has found a good cheap Bodega wine. Little Angelino came here one night with another waiter (spare Sunday barman) with 10-litre (!) demijohn of his Bodega wine and I threw 1 chair, 1 mop, 1 cushion out the window, and Angelino fell $2\frac{1}{2}$ metres down, returning home not sober, as he had arrived.

At times I don't eat for 2-3 days, then food (the thought) takes on its true holy nature. One eats and feels like weeping. Like loving you, except I feel like laughing. I mean silently, internally, cat-laughter, risible, ha. Stout Rafaelito, known as The Onion, says my nature is *sospechoso*.

Do you know Swift's *Journal to Stella*? It has an invented love-language in it. She had a bad complexion, so had he; they may have been secretly married, although he didn't attend her funeral. When I begin to refer to writers (dead) and the awful act of writing, it's a sure sign that I am getting tired.

Fitz

Letter 11

Copenhagen,
1. july 1975

My beloved
Received you letter (not you) days ago.

My beloved, next time ravens visit you then dream then dream, don't fight them follow them untill you are wit-scared yourself and inaccessible for others but not for me. I love you more and more fervently. That you must know. That I must tell you. I don't know if it will do any good for you or if it will do anything for you at all but so it is. "I knew you were violent that your love would be difficult." Yes. You are indeed not either the most simple being in this world. Sometimes I'm so afraid that you suffer too much. Sometimes you've hinted that you were through but I don't quite believe you.

I send you a longer letter in next week where I hopefully have vacasion. I'm very busy this weeks, maybe I finish my

41

steady job and try to earn money only by radio-work and tv-text. Everything is hanging together, I cannot continue like before, you made me longing for the dangerous. Don't fear that I'm really insane, I make it slowly and with a certain plan in my head.

I'm always thinking of you always missing you, do never anything without imagine you observing me, warming me by your look at it. Often I miss you too bitterly, our long long kiss and your slowly attentive moves inside me ... and my answers. Other love like rabbits comparing to you. Are rabbits. Only you are my only real man. I miss our butterfly-game, pleasure pleasure and deadly serious and our sombre painfull love I need too, the reverse on the pleasure, that which hurted, was nearly impossible. If I was together with you I would cultivate that too, keep us in the painfull. "Never go into a bad temper," you once said in the kitchen. O, I would do that, look at ravens from any possible angle, touch the metallic, cloth feathers open the yellow bad (and empty) beak and keep the blinking eyes untill one of us looked away.

I write you a good telling letter from Bornholm my beloved Island (much more than Rørvig), next week where I have TIME which is so important as LOVE.

Elin

Letter 12

Goatshed, 1st July 75

My dearest Elin,
Very sticky times, the summer come in, Goatshed roasting, family here, much noise, all topsy-turvey, no peace, all argument, money running out rapidly but have just been saved, sold by ingenious letter MSS to University that buys my stuff, breathing space until end of summer I hope. Family here a week today, last Tuesday went with Larry at 5:30 am after all-night chess with Wittgenstein to Malaga, where they had been since 5:00 am., two hours early, no sign of them at Bar Alameda Colon. I went to station where I had very

peculiar search in very hot morning for shed where your heavy parcel was handed over to me at reasonable charge of 35 pesetas, last money I had. Walked up and down rails and was mis-directed here and there, and at long last found a little office in a long storeroom where some officials were not in the least surprised to see me at last, and pushed across ledger to sign.

I opened it here, troubled day, startled by contents, not a couple of shirts as imagined (before I lifted heavy parcel), but everything I wanted: the thin paper ream, the folders, clipboard, all most useful and very handsome, almost German, but even better. I am so pleased to have them. The shirt is much admired, except by my wife. I washed it in the little river we never went to, below Canillas cemetery and dump Gehenna, smoking, went to that bar where a bull was in process of being killed on television. Since then your photos arrived with you rather far away. Your flat looks very fancy, and you in white very regal; all those pictures behind, and that Trunk. If only you would come closer. What is that you are drinking? Are you dreaming of me, because your white shirt seems to be rolling up and some buttons undoubtedly undone? I see how brown you are, what a beautiful woman, most of the humour of your face is missing, some of it in the darker ones (early morning or late at night, or that in-between-time: middle-of-the-Copenhagen-night?). Steffen looks like Polanski. I hope he has not the instincts of that dangerous Polack.

Please send me the photos of yourself naked on your bed,* I'm quite sure you are more beautiful than Goya's Duchess of Alba, who gave poor Goya a terrible time one winter. I think all the Horrors of War came from that winter: he turned against women, became vengeful, his pictures teemed with hags, women running with lifted skirts to see soldiers pass. He did a painting of her all insolence in black, pointing to Goya's name on the sand at her feet; her hand level with her crotch, a much more erotic painting than the famous lady in bed, whose trunk is wrong, the position of one breast impossible. You

---

* Have told my wife about you and what I feel for you, in a sort of self-induced storm, when I thought I was going insane. Had to tell her.

naked in forest or beach would be better than that punitive lady who soured Goya so much (I think he was sour anyway).

I am typing this at the end of a sticky troublesome day, just to thank you for such a useful parcel. It was very much your gift, surprising me (once again); very much our sort of times—the search for it, humorous, and hot. Can I say I miss you? No one else is you in bed. I have been thinking that you must come to London in September. How long can you have? I am in a big hole of debt but I cannot worry about that. When I think of you, another sort of life is there, begins, continues, a better time. Invited to campo and squeamish sons horrified to see rabbit killed before their eyes, knife plunged in, all fur and life one minute the next just skin and eyes. My dearest.

(Unsigned)

PS: Other page not what I wished to say, I continue now in order to try and be calm, invoking you my dear calms me, the idea that you exist somewhere is a good calming feeling. A breeze comes in through the flyscreen and it's my thought of you: you are my calmness.

Had a sort of brainstorm on the path to Santa Anna and feared I was going mad, could not let Coppera touch me; all the ideas in my head were rushing into me and away and I with them. It was most alarming. I thought my reason was going for good. Then I told her about you, weeping, holding stones. I said I would not allow myself to think of you. C. said, Go on, think of her. It was like protecting you—not thinking of you.

My disappointment grows without you, walking before me. I had Kneppen with C. in the pool but it wasn't any good. Will you come to London and live with me a little in September? There are woods there. I don't like the place too much. You might change that. I miss giving you big tips, miss sinking into you, miss your eyes, and your German love lingo. I feel very disappointed without you. Isn't it strange that it comes in this way with such force? I use your ribbon, wear your sandals, in the evening wear your Indian shirt. Larry Rivers looks at it and says That's a very fine shirt. Miss Mouse looks at me and hardly recognizes it. It's the part of you in me they see. They know me very well. She was the one I went to bed with after you, nothing *Kneppen* happened, it was no good; there was nothing in it for her or me, because you were there. You are in me; have possessed me. I miss your voice. Your voice tells me that there is no madness.

I hear voices, and no one is there. The church bell speaks to me, a threat. I hear Wittgenstein guffawing in the kitchen with Coppera, and he isn't there. I am trembling on the roof because he has come to take my wife and family away from me. He offers me a house at the mouth of the Ganges in a place called Chittagong; from there you can see dead dogs floating out into the Indian Ocean. I say, I don't want anything to do with your Shittygong; and make my escape over the roof. This book is full of water. For the first time I face myself, face my face; it's full of passing bells and corpses making their last journey.

Perhaps it's my dead mother who is writing it, holding my hand. She always wanted to write a book. Or my father who should have been a poet but was an idiot instead, facing nothing all his life. He used to lift me up at windows and point out strange things outside: his lost poetry. I never did that for my own children because I wanted to keep the poetry to myself, how selfish.

Your presents touched me so much. If you go to bed with another Knepp, my amulet will either choke you or break or catch fire. I'd like to have a colour photo of you wearing it naked. Once I had Hannelore wear a wristwatch around her ankle when she was naked. It was very strange to see.

But you tearing me, tearing into me, softening me, hardening me until I cannot bear it, perhaps you are a witch, the last Danish witch come to torment the last Irish, so Irish I cannot live there, can't live anywhere, except perhaps in you. When one dives too deeply into water the head crackles like an aluminium basin, and when one thinks too deepy it does the same, although strictly speaking I do not think at all. The book is full of people diving; most come up again.

CHAPTER 5: Letter 13

On the Rørvig Ferry

Letter 13

Sunday evening,
the 6th of July 1975
Copenhagen.

My dearest —

Copenhagen is very hot in this weeks. Steffen has taken care of Marijke all the weekend, I needed very much to be alone, have been busy with idiotic things the last weeks, everything at home was one Big Mess, not a clean plate, nothing clean cloth. I've been in one of my eternal recomming depression periods, when it is extra difficult to pretend effectiv,—I'm far-off, cannot get out of my own figment imagination, the same themes turn and grow and change but are still the same, a kaleidoscope of inner confusion. Now I am through the outside mess and have used the rest of the weekend to try to make fair copy of bewildered notes during the week and it became definitely bad: a row of highflown inexact words, neither prose nor poetry, without genuine sensations, a row of oldfashioned assertions which do not hit. I am very depressed. If I never learn to write properly I cannot nothing in this world. I am clever to nothing, nothing at all. It is all approats, giving up, making dreams, useless dreams, hoping a little again ...

I complain. I promised myself never to complain to you and especialy not about this matter. Now I have done. Now I have been a native woman thrown out of white man's tent because of bad manners.

In a way I remember you so well. Your brightness. Is anything called that? I can't stand to use the dictionary all the time. My only force is to make guess, hope they fit somebody, something. Thinking things over they disappear to me.

Intellectual thing at least. They must come as a cut or they vanish as you say. You give me new words, too, I could fall in love in english. Sometimes I'm going to do. When I'm thinking over feelings they don't vanish. Oppersite, they crows. Because you don't think feelings, I guess. How can I live my life? Who is paying for dreams? Why do I need food? Why do I need *things*? (That damned things). Why do I not live on a greek island? Why is the world so sluggish a material? Down again:

Why can't I make it light?

I am ashame to complain. Will do it again and again. Tell me to shut up.

10/7: You say nothing about *I Ching*? Nonsense for you? (Old stuff hanging over Elin's head). Steffen always laugh when I absorbed (dictionary) of that kind of matter. But contempt me too, think it is a complicated and childish 'stage-setting (dictionary) or rather depriving (dictionary) of a obvious reality, understandable for a child of five. Same Steffen get me to laugh so heartily and painfull (in danish: *hjerteligt og smerteligt*, a thorough-fucked-wordpair) the other day when he said: When you feel your thoughts to collect to complaint then beat your head into the wall. I'm beating my head into the wall now. Again. Oh I miss you. Again. Forgive me my love that I miss you so much. Just red your mad letter again (Fitz-again-Fitz-Fitz-again), long parts without rest, I think I mean stop, pause, long breath, fading out and starting again, long breath from a love which wants to empty both body and mind. How can you write like that, how can you do it against us, how can you make me suffering that much? Sometimes I'm catched by a great anger to you, to demand, no to give the feeling of present but still you are not here, to prevent me to live here by keeping me there, I am longing and prevented, I am kept in imagination and must drown myself in home-made wine and over-excitement, sometimes I'm catched by a great anger to you. Then it disappears and I must laugh to myself.

(Unsigned)

Rørvig.
Marijke and I go to Rørvig about every second weekend. First

we take a normal Inter-City-train, then a little provincial train to *Hundested* (meaning Place of Dogs) (??) which is a little harbourtown on the coast of northzeeland. To get out of the train in Hundested is every time a lovely surprise, the air is clear, the sea as always, the harbour modest.

Then we take a ferry, clumsy as a clog, to Rørvig. I always feel cruising among the greek islands. Marijke talks. She always does. In Rørvig my parents are waiting. They are glad to see me, I am glad to see them, Marijke is very glad. The journey takes a little more than two hours.

We walk home (10 minutes) to the little summerhouse, about 40 years old, dark trees, window boxes even if we are in the middle of nature. ("Im Freien" lovely pianopieces by Bartok). Rørvig is a Holiday-center, lovely nature, victims little butter-hole, the innocence's last chanal to a little reality, a little plants, a little owner-feeling. Very much like my parents are, very well-selected. The beatch still has its wildness, is very beautifull and pure. I use the weekend to wash and iron, wash hair, talk with my parents, sleep, cut the grass for my father, go to the beatch with Marijke on my fathers old high bike (why bar on gentleman-bikes?), look at television in the evening, go for walks with Marijke and drink a beer at the inn (which is placed by the main-road). My parents would die by annoyance because of the extra-money, one could drink that beer at home in the garden ... well, they don't see the pleasure in a polished pub-glass and a perfect temperature of beer and the easiness of being in a public place out of the home, the sacrosant home.—I talked very much with my parents, never lie to them, tell them "everything" but edit my reality.

At the beatch with Marijke:
Marijke is naked, I've very little black bathing drawers, my 12 years old nephew's. I had forgotten bathing suit in Copenhagen, he has forgotten these in Rørvig. I adapt myself to the sand, preparing meeting you. You come slowly with little floating standstills in between. I don't go far into it, people around, Marijke around, but it is difficult to stop. And difficult to go on to the absolute end. ("We didn't make love enough, far from ..." didn't refer to something numerically but to the abandonment, the courage). Marijke is running

48

around, they fits so beautiful, the sea and her, I try to keep the picture, not making any thinking around it. She is collecting shells in an empty Nescafe glass. She meets a boy. You know how children meet each other and stop, to the extreme watchful, super-animals, sniff with all senses. Then Marijke with an abrupt move casts all the shells at his feet and goes away. Sometimes I'm wondering myself, that Marijke in one hand gives me so much but in the other I could leave her tomorrow, calm, if I knew she was growing well without me.

I went for a walk alone. Went on a narrow highlevelled path through sand-mountains with pines, brooms and wild roses. I was tempty to go down into the green valley but went on at the narrow path in assurance that something fantastic must be found by the end of it. I went carefully, I'm so clumsy, hidden treeroots under the sand (take care not to dream so you fall, take care not to fall so you must stop dreaming). The air was mild with cold streams plaited in, the bees was humsing; following the less resistance (can I assert that? Like that appeared to me). I felt awake and happy.—And yet I was disturbed by something, somewhat punctured the lovely picture, an unrest which didn't come from myself, and when I came to the end of the road I saw what it was: It was the limitation.

Nearly all over in Denmark you feel the houses with people just beside you, the houses are waiting just around the corner, voices turn up, you don't know from where and when and how many but you know, that only a limit area is preserved, only a quiet limit area have somebody in the city at a meeting decided to preserve—When innocence confuse with an unbroken hymen the point is lost.

I am glad friday evening when I arrive and glad sunday evening when I leave. Rørvig is a lovely place. Exploited, yes, summerhouses close together, but there is still a kind of innocence, a fragile middle-class innocence, open to rape I'm afraid. A Holiday-center. A place without necessity, without power of resistance. A hobby. Like my father, so kind in his stupidity and like my mother, so clever in her presentiments and so stupid in her fear, her denying. I love my parents, have tenderness for them. They are innocent.

My Fitzy—these are lines from the beginning of the

summer (26.6.), started as a letter for you, turned out something else, now I've tried to translate most of it, it is very difficult. Hope you have a picture now from Rørvig and not only another monologue from Elin.

9. july, daytime

I'm sick today, have diarré—comical so physical everything must turn—I go into closed doors and have just overturned my coffee all over the desk. I am so weak in hands that I couldn't type if not I knew I could and I couldn't walk if not the walking already was invented. Strange that you are not afraid at all for a meeting again. I'm so afraid of London, prefer thousand Ireland in October, but I cannot do anything but what you want. So much you have loved Hannelore, love her, I knew all the time, also in Atepmoc, that you loved her, have a room in you for Hannelore only, a boudoir (Ophelia's bedroom) and a sittingroom for Coppera. What room have you got for me?

There are figures predestined, a figure, one that fits your inner pictures—by destiny you loved Hannelore. The figure imagined and by free choice taken—that was me. Jung calls this Anima and Animus. I was only your Animus. Hannelore was your true love, your Anima. You made yourself love me, but you had to love Hannelore. This I am afraid is the truth.

The answer is near but I will not put it myself. The name for me I love, variations over the same theme, the old theme: Annelise (also in *Torn og Engle*), Hannelore, Anna, Hannel, I feel jealous and happy and proud, the dance is not a stupid, selfish, personal pair-dance (its shape is like that, but don't misunderstand it), really it is a chain-dance, it makes me elevated by happiness and crushed by envie, cannot choose to be whore or—I look in the dictionary, as usual you haven't the word, something between priest and witch.

I love the name Anna. The walk for Santa Anna and the closed el-house with the open door, a walk so beautifull, so tender, nearly langourous. I was thinking of Italy while I walked and saw the green landscape, thin earth upon eternal stones and therefore so delighted. I don't use the dictionary now, do you at all understand what I mean? I remember the yellow bush, a striking an octave higher than the rest of the sinfonie.

NEVER MORE I want to hear who you are fucking at the Third River with the deep smooth vessel. There are so many places in the world,—why the Third River? I fling my sorrow back: Your amulet didn't break or turned in a blaze. I took it off. You are trembling by the thought of Coppera with him you call Wittgenstein? I understand that. Poor poor everybody to whom this happen. Was Coppera trembling when you left her?

Sorry you didn't like the pictures. I'm not surprised, they were postcards. An impossible situation with the pictures, so much trouble already, promiscuity in an odd way to hunt love-signs of yourself. Yes, the dark pictures are from the *bleu heur* at Steffen's terasso. I don't send the naked one.

Strange so often you mention Knud Andersen, your instincts are sure, you remind of him, the same limpid selfishness without any wickedness. He was blond with blue eyes, you are dark with green eyes, it gives the differens.

Your letter scared me. I know that it will scare me lesser in a couple of days when I've red it more times. But I know too, that the sight of you and the dream I dreamt after will be lying, always attensive, in the back of my head. However there is nothing to complain, I knew it, had expected it, wondering when it came, I saw it in the very second in Pepinos bar. I saw in your eyes that point where longing and fear are meeting each other. Have a meeting.

Strange passionate over-used words. My scribbling is the same for the moment, I have no other words in this weeks, I look at my "poems" and I'm paralysed by their impossibleness, ridiculousness. "When they come back often enough they become careless." Yes. Like that it is. I presume. I don't know it, never reach that distance, am like a child, in it or out of it, burning or forgetting, absorbed or not caring. *My ambitions groan.* Oh yes. That also why I lived so well with you: I had no language to force you into my problems. I became only body and soul with you, no spirit. The difference between soul and spirit. "Old stuff hanging over Elin's head." I love you. I fear you.

(Unsigned)

PS: About Wrong placed longings. You say: "they are not wrong placed for I have them for you too."

Sweet Fitzy, a touching mis-understanding. That was exactly what I ment: we have towards each other, and *that* is maybe the mistake itself. I discovered once that the romantic way of thinking ("to long for each other") started exactly when the religious way of thinking stopped. And therefore may all this love-feelings among modern people are mis-placed (religious) feelings ... do you not understand?

How can you hear difference between *floating* (air) and *flowzing* (water)???

You can! I just invented a "z". But how do you choose?

According to the dictionary, which I love and hate, it is the same. English is to me a very Floating-flowing language. A bee hums and a humsing man does the same (when he sings silently). A nice word-game is lost by taking the consequence immediately and call it the same. Well, english is not floating here—I better stop criticize your language!

7/7/75

My everday

The watch calls half past seven. Every morning I try not to fall asleep again but use the time between half past seven and eight to get the habit of life again. But often I'm very tired and fall asleep again anyway and wake up, confused, five minutes to eight. Marijke is able to do nearly anything herself, brush teeth, dress herself (surprising clothes together, and so much clothes ... lots of clothes, taken off again later in the day, brought home from the kindergarten by me in a big paper-bag). We have not really breakfast, none of us can eat in the morning. I paint my face, arrange myself, adapt myself so I'm half eat-able for myself and the surroundings. Without make-up I'm very rough, wild. I feel my own face more wellknown with make-up than naked. In the moderated version there comes a tenderness which I also have. Indeed.

Then we drive, Marijke behind on my cycle. When we are in good time we stop at a certain baker and buy 2 yougurt, just across Rosenborg Slot, we have a bench where we eat breakfast. People pass by, not many, and cars pass by (more) and maybe think that we don't belong to the slaves of time, but we do anyway.

Then Marijke wants me to tell about Rosenborg Slot which is built by king Christian the Fourth in sixteenhundred-somewhat (renaissance-Castle). He was in love with a hard and beautifull woman called Kirstine Munk, who let him down in his oldness, riding around with a guardsman instead, and let the king die alone with dropsy in his legs. Marijke doesn't mind the same and same story, but I move longer and longer from the fact which are so unsure anyway. Beside that she will come to school once and have her learning made correct there.

Then I arrive a little too late at my work and drink coffee. The dreams of the night throw long shadows in the late morning, I do not quite awake until later. The post and the nervousity of the day arrive, a dubble nervousity, a real terror for having done—or not done—something irreparable (I neither own general view nor memory, there is lacks in my scratched intelligence) and another kind of nervousity, a secret excitement, an expectation which selden have name and face (but have it now) and which is laying, trembling under everything. The most of my days goes with hiding or re-establish that I'm never quite attentive, not even when I really try, that I always in one way or another are thinking of something else. When I'm working on my own things other kind of horrors come in: doubt, hopelessness, incapability but never inattention. When I was with you I sometimes be melancholy but never nervous, there was never this gulf between acting and thinking or what I did and what I ought to do.

I'm the best looking girl here, or rather maybe, that girl with most effect. (About my beauty you are talking: I know of course that I *look like* a beautifull girl, that I *seem* to be clever, but I know too, that ... well). Because I look like a beautifull girl there is attention around me. That I enjoy in all its craching schizophrenia.

11 o'clock I'm mad by thirst and buy a light beer (without alcohol), a buying everybody percieve correct as beginning of alcoholism, still ashamed to be what it is. I'm moving very fast, forget my purse in the canteen and things like that. Half

past twelve I eat lunch, sometimes alone at my office if the persons in the canteen look too dull but mostly I stay trying to charm my superior to doubt that I'm so incapable they all the time are just going to discover.

Between four and five o'clock I take my bike and go for Marijke in kindergarten. Often we are both rather tired and rather hungry and sit down on a bench on "Strøget" (the main-walking-street in Copenhagen) eating icecream instead of making important buyings or we go to Steffen's terasse and let an hour crumble away. Everything are closing at half past five sharp. Only selden I'm in time to what I ought, only I am behind in tax, toiletpaper, dishing etc. When we are at home about 6 o'clock I make tea, doing house-things, making food. Half past seven we eat, mostly very simple: potatos, salat, sometimes bacon, milk for Marijke, wine for me (I make the wine myself). In this weeks we are eating strawberry, lots of them, they are expensive but we love them. (Strawberry, oesters and an irish poet and I shouldn't complaint).

After dinner I make Cafe con Leche, still missing the goatmilk and the 103. In between these things I write to you or myself, it's the same, but Marijke hates that. She wants to talk. Much banal chattering with surprises in between.

Yesterday she told me that angels had haloes in order to find their way in the nighttimes when they are flying in the heavens. Also she told me newly: My mother is dangerous like a crocodile! At nine o'clock a long bed-ritual starts, she doesn't sleep before about ten o'clock, has never belonged to the much-sleeping children.

Then I am myself with a daylong need for *wasting the time*. I have a very big need for wasting time. I sit down on my bed, neither read nor write. I'm looking out in the air and dream. The pictures, the situations are pouring in, mostly very banal, difficult to use to anything. I hardly can stop. Late, at 11 o'clock when I ought to go to bed, I'm free and laughing at the pattern I've been running in all the day and which necesarity I cannot break only fulfill or not fulfill. In these hours I'm happy, filled with optimism, trustfull and believing in long chains of days of this color. Then I feel young again, that I'm just on the start of all of it, that I in the next moment "around the next corner will be able to fly."

That's me, my love. What do you say?—I laugh.—No matter what even you (the most precious thing I have in these times) say: the things are like they are.

8th July 1975

For some weeks I cycled a detour while I was on my way to work. Not by the fifth watery quadrilateral, a pond in a park, our bench of the mornings between two churches. Then the old church Vartorv, then the Kanal, Amager Boulevard, the bridge over Stydhavn, cycling close to the water by the flowering chestnut trees, to Islands Brygge quayside. In fact I hadn't time, would be late and was it, but I was a little happy, didn't know why. The way I choosed is ugly: a dusty by-pass-way a little outside the centre of the town (Artillivej), with little dying factories, football-grass, workships, hutments from the time of war and allotments, insane in their care for flagstaffs and geraniums. The way end in a Clondyke.

Suddenly a miraculous stream of scent come to meet me and up from a high hoarding I saw roses, faint-pink roses, lots of kilograms roses, thirty metres roses hanging, climing ... scented released roses. I felt blessed and plucked three of them and put them in a beer-glass on my desk. 10 o'clock a letter arrived, a letter from you, the mad letter, the letter which is one breath.

Since I haven't had time to bike that way, have put it off, thinking of it but not touching it. This day, this morning I turned, without knowing it, to the left and suddenly I was on that road again. The roses scented still more strong than before, many were died, the last ones overbearing. Carefully I took three again, put them in the glass. They scent scent scent, and a half time ago your letter arrived, even my instincts you have given back to me.

Sometimes I have that feeling that we are writing or thinking the same things in the same days, that we are in the same moods in the same periods, a lovestory conducted not in fake-german but by somebody else, I feel how the transport of the letters brings a artificial shifting in a congruence (?) which is present. A letter arrived. A answer to my unmailed letter.

9. July, in the night

Red your letter fast, hunting for love-signs, understood it this night, had a horrofic dream now in the very early morning. I've written it down in danish, show it to you a day we can bear it. Strange strange, I've been catched in such a anxiety on your behalf (an anxiety beside my own) just in that days you went that brain-storming-walk with Coppera. Much more than anxiety, a fearfull danger, yes. I fear I've invoked it over us, know it is nonsense, you have all the ghosts inside yourself, but maybe I've made them awake.

What are we going to do? My dreams said: The ghosts take over the power, the power you invoked *for your own happiness* turns against you and swallow you. Like the pearls and the pigs. How do I dare to write to you, to tell you that you must follow the ravens? How do I dare when I must know that it demands a power I don't know if I have? Moreover in my arrogance imagine that I've strength enough for two, for both of us? for you too.

Never trust me. Use what you can. Never trust me.

No, I don't go to Holmens Kirkegaard anymore. Did in my childhood (we lived 4 streets away) when my mother thought I was in school and the school thought I was ill at home (well, then I was lying then. Is it the world to blame or me to blame that everything isn't possible to say without saying the opperset just after?). Then—when I was a lying child—I went to Holmens Kirkegaard but more often to Statens Museum for Kunst. The attendants knew me, wondered I guess, but never asked, talked to me about the pictures as attendants love to do. I was listening but wanted them to go, was then still more greedy about loneliness than now. I loved the room to the left with the Matisse-pictures, such a kind sensualism. Now everything is changed, the museum rebuilt, very elegant.

I must stop now, I hardly can't stop talking to you when I begin. Steffen and I talked for 12 years, now there is silence between us, we comfort each other a little, when we see the other one is suffering. We never go to bed with each other. He would like it, I know, but for me it has been impossible since it became impossible. "Can I say I miss you?" Can I? I look at your first letter. In order to get the habit, you said. We got the habit. I got. I have no other habit in fact. Tell me why you are like smiling when you put down something sad about me.

I have found a possible way to see you in London. First I bristled by aversion against the thought of London and the flat there. I had Dublin and Buswells Hotel and Galway and the mill and our walking in the valleys and our accidently guestroom, always unforgetable, and tender, a little blunt conversations in the evenings with our intellectual host, you and he in fictitious disagreement, your brain-drill, I listening and not-listening, and then our (other) drill, invented on the spot, difficult, incalculable, sweetnessing until the uneatable, and bitter to the unrecognized and german lovewords like fizzy wine in between and with dreadfull expanses of doubt and—more dreadfull—emptyness. First I had all this in my mind. But I must do as you say as long as I have to. I cannot help that. Not now. Early enough I will be myself again.

Now I see myself walking up the steps (you must not come and pick me up, no airport, no taxidrivers, no suitcase-mess. I will not walk in that staircase together with you, that staircase Coppera and your sons has been running in for years). You let the frontdoor unlocked. I go in and put my suitcase in the hall (and lock). You must not come out to me. The way to you I find by following the open doors. I walk around in the flat, you hear me, I'm not coming at once. You are sitting in your workingroom (I suppose) you are sitting in your chair or laying on your bed or swimming on the floor or hanging on the wall. You are in that room you have been in thousand times before. The only omen is a rustling which as well could come from a clumsy Poltergeist who anyway is thrown out from the society because of its unspiritual noisiness. You still have the last red words in your ear when you feel my lips on your neck. You are surprised. I am there so suddenly as a bee in the Spring, humsing, as you say. There is no transition and not any distance between our absence and presence. The time between the airport in Malaga and our new touch, our repeated touch is only an outer assertion, sweeped off the tablecloth like crumbs. Vanished. E.

CHAPTER 6: Letters 14, 15

Sailing to Bornholm
(Matterly Light)

Letter 14

Goatshed
Friday 18th July 75

My dearest,

Your long (6th July, Sunday evening, 8th, daytime 9th, 10th & 13th July, "My everyday" and "Rørvig") turbulent, scandalous letter arrived yesterday in the great heat, and I have just re-read it with my hair standing on end.

My "brightness", as you are pleased to call it, is but a reflection, and pale at that, of the great pleasure I take in you. It makes me so glad that glad is hardly the word, hardly enough—hence the smile at your unhappiness, because I know it's something I can correct, can cure. You lift me up. You do, you really do, so I have to smile—if that makes any sense to you. Your letters are breathing into me, your breath in my mouth, your extraordinary eyes watching me, waiting for me. One turbulent fluidum.

Marijke sounds very like a small version of you, which is probably why I like her, my idea of her, always talking. Angels flying by night, with halos on! My youngest son, Ben, is like that. He caught a swallow the other day, had it on his shoulder, was its mother, kept it for a night, catching flies for it, feeding it, letting it off the terrace in the morning. It was called Chick. He sent it to heaven he said, made sure it gets there, by looking at it with slanted eyes, seeing it in a blur. All things and persons he regards like that will get to heaven, all meet in heaven. His brothers, Coppera, me. He greatly regrets not sending a grasshopper, which he had for five hours, to heaven in that way. The grasshopper is damned.

Yes, I believe in I CHING if you do. Meant to ask Larry Rivers for the thing. I only suggested London because

September is not so long away (and you reproach me with being too patient). You would never find that flat. You take the BEA coach and it goes for maybe an hour along the most depressing highway (the Great North Road or some such grand name) in all creation. Then you go down into the most stinking Tube full of people who are bludgeoned out of life, or others crazy as grasshoppers. The Tube train stops and starts maybe 26 times, for 50 minutes or more, going North (so it must have been the Great West Road you came in on), at Finsbury Park you follow the street map, the street-door of the flat is operated by buzzer, the flat is right at the top, and I am there, or part of me, and a bed is there and champagne in the fridge, and the shakes begin all over again.

Perhaps your idea of Ireland in October might be better. May and October are the best months there. Galway is nice, great gulps of the Atlantic, extraordinary clouds, the people almost Spanish in their good manners—some of the Armada fleet washed up there one wet August, survivors being stripped by the natives, then slaughtered by the English. I could work through September, get my finances in order, if that is possible. My agent is arranging a meeting with publisher and I, talking turkey. He wants a big advance on novel so that I can stop worrying about ££. It worries me like a dog with a rat, shaking it, shaking life out of it.

We should begin again in some peculiar place.

Galway would do for a beginning—the journey across Ireland you would like. They have a bar on the train. Galway comes up in the evening with huge banks of clouds. We could go to the Aran Isles. We could take off. We could. How lucky I am to have met you; so that I can believe that again. Put on your amulet again.

I am lying all the time, except to you. And to myself, not lying. I spent my childhood in a state of semi-terror, and later too. Now it's got used to me: we can get along, Terror and I. (I see you as a Lying Child in Holmens Kirkegaard: you are picking three roses, hunting for love signs. You are the best-looking girl in the DR. They all want to go to bed with you, Bogen and Carlsen and Andersen, and I can't blame them). Now I've trapped all the ghosts in a bottle and swallowed the bottle, it's only a small phial full of ghosts, gibbering away.

Yes, we are writing the same things and thinking the same things on the same day. I see nothing much of the you I remember well in those photos, no. I'll wear your belt, I'll buy new pants, I'll light your candle. I'm your Spanish invention alright, and you mine. They have dug up the square. Fat Luis is in heaven. I never go to Aurelio's. My kids collect the post. I half-live, working, looking at insects, waiting, biding my time, try not to think of you too much. You are there, dreaming in me, weeping in me, laughing in me. Damn Knud Andersen. And Bogen after him. I press my lips on you, you open to me, I give you slow Big Tip, I give you fast BT, I lie in you, I die and come to life again in you. How strange that is!

I end here. Paul posts this tomorrow. Have a good vacation. Think about Galway in October. Type your envelopes, my address I mean.

(It came to my mind the other day: you in djalaba in the kitchen, looking most beautiful. I put my hands into the pocket onto you skin: how strange the feel of your skin. You were laughing.)

(Unsigned)

Letter 15

21. july 1975
Copenhagen

Dearest Fitzy,

Came from Bornholm with ship this morning. I visited two quite different kinds of friends, replying two outerlying points in myself. For some years ago I got surprised and sad when my friends saw each other as idiots and then I understood the system.

On Bornholm there are two repeated names: Koefod (cowfoot) and Sildehoved (herring-head), Aase and Finn Sildehoved are very close friends to me. I've known Aase for 15 years but actually she wasn't my friend untill she a sudden day (to horror of everybody) married a COOK from Bornholm: Finn! Before she was mistress (and niece) to elder friend of Steffen and me. Finn looks like a cherub and has a hoarse voice (struma as child), he is a bit confused in head and with unpleasant ambition of being intellectual. Nevertheless he is one of the finest, most delicate persons I know, one of the difficult types who is word-blind, not orthographical but in their expresses, their choice of words. You must find a certain dictionary in order to understand what he means. When you understand that you discover that he is seeing the most delicate connections.

Aase and Finn live in a messy house, a hotel once, with Lea, a fearfull witch of 6 and the offering-child Janus 4 years old. I love them for their sense of living, for their downright way of living. They do (nearly) as they say. It is rather rare, I think. We up-value (??) the gifts of each other, it is rather euforizing (Can you say that?). Meaning getting high.

The other friends I visited, Anne and Peter, are smart persons. The girl is very lovely (ex-model), the man is a beaf. I disgust him. Anne has a pure-hearted cynism I cannot resist, she is very quick-witted and have a sense of reality in this ambitious, neurotic milieu which I admire very much. She is scolding me for being occult, Aase is scolding me for living an exterior life.

Bornholm is filled with promises.

Bornholm

We drive in a car or walk on a road and all the time you see places or lightings, lightnings or something you don't actually see at all, but you feel desire for going closer, to go into it or take it in hands. We drived for a tour one day, Finn and I and the children and found a spot in a hardwood with this movable light I like so much. The children tickled us with flowering grass. Lea, the eldest, the most conscious, tickled me at the thighs and nipples, the mood was of the most delightfull erotic character, we (the grown up) remembered the innocence, an abundance of sweetness without aim.

On our way home we drived through a wood of pines with this special brown/lillac light in the nealless underwood and immediately after through a hardwood, halfopen and moistful, covered with moss on stones and stems (like the wings in the theaterperformance from the childhood you know) and then a birch-grove, nearly only light (silver and gold actually), an icon from a pantheist-religion and then the mainroad in front of you with grey stone-dikes and bittersmelling fields from yellow mustardflowers.

And the light, so matterly, always broken always reminding that light is colour—all colour. Potentially. I guess this is a special island-light which you maybe know from Ireland. Bornholm is a little island only 40 miles on each side, a rocky-island with stone-formations and nakedness too. You cannot drive around for more than 10 minutes before you have a meeting again with the sea, the sea in front of you, below you.

A calm came to me in this days. I know that the physical milieu means a great deal to the mental state but in those days my respect for the surroundings has grown or rather ratified, maybe. To be on the right place is to rig your sails properly, never settle down on the wrong place, it is very important to live and not only survive. So many things found their place in this days, my restlessness vanished. My fear for being that person you hope, that one you wish, that one you can use—this fear, too, was fading out in this honest surrounding because it is a false fear (false to worry about). After you put me in the plane in Malaga I've had a time full of missing and turmoil, first a melancholy so I could hardly breath, then desperation so I can hardly stay in my own skin, then a kind of anger: what are my wage for all this suffer? and then, last, a fear: Oh yes, what *are* my wage going to be ... I've been unsure and disturbed because you never answer that part of my letters which is not about my erotic feelings for you, I saw (see) it as an aversion to that part of me which try to understand everything happened to me, try to make morales (not neccesary moralities).

This "refusing," as I called it, hurted me a bit but does it lesser and lesser. Because I love you more and more, focussing myself to love you, to follow you. I see that one must love by surplus. You made me awake, how I use this awakeness is a privatecase. You have learnt me, my beloved Fitzy, to shut up. Well ... I cannot assert that with all this words, but you have shown me that silence is a possibility, maybe an extraordinary one. No word is so pure as to kiss you.

I've feared the silence between us after all this letters, seen it as a stop, an emptyness. But it will not be so. I am looking forward to my german love-language and my simple messages, I am looking forward to have no language. I am trustfull both to you and myself, I feel—if I'm listening very much and translate you, not from english to danish, but to the deepest meaning I'm able to see—I feel that maybe I can be a little happy and maybe—who knows—make you a little happy. So your answer can come true: "I saw happiness in you."

Elin

PS: Practical: The Pastor and his wife might come home telling you that Steffen don't know at all you are my beloved. But he does. I was on toilet and he (Steffen) couldn't resist to ask Pernille: "Tell me, who is this Irish fellow?" They both reacted very quick and correct.

CHAPTER 7: Letters 16, 17, 18

The Floating Trousseau

Letter 16

24. July 1975
Copenhagen, thursday night

Mein liebe Liebling, mein Kind und Brüderlein, mein Dicht und Wirklichkeit, mein Angst und Freue, my Fitz.

Just received your letter. Read my "epistle" from Bornholm, remember my new name and understand that you have done it again, catched me in my heart, beating me in my stomack, taken the air out from my lungs. You called me Anna Bornholm.

You have done it again. You have seen me again, seen me as I am (can be), you have lighted me through again, you are a seeing person, seeing me anyway. Oh, *Gott!*

I love every word in your letter, letters. A psychoanalist would tear his hair because of your determining of erotic, your picture of me in this fixing-bath, your Big Tips. I've never met anything like that, you even surpass Knud Andersen. I cannot quite recognize myself but if you see me like that, I may be like that, must turn to be like that.—

Your smile made sense to me, help me so much. What a promise.—I was never jealous of Hannel, knew all the time that you haven't loved her, that you had tenderness for her but she was a spare-love. Is it cruel to say? I knew she had been the wife of the Pastor and even in separated it hints certain limits in her. No, I was never jealous of Hannel. For Coppera, I have blended feelings. I perceive her, actually, as very sympathetical, beautifull and intelligent, too, but obviously wrong for you. As me in my Steffen, apart from that we are through the hate. But I am very jealous of her. You have had your youth together with her, you have been together with her on the impossible beds of your youth and have wished—more fervently than ever since in your life—to make love to her. You

64

(F&C) have had the trust together about you as a famous writer and herself as a beautifull woman in company with gifted men, men who everybody saw was secret in love with her Coppera Fitzgerald. And you have had the kids together. It alarms me that you still quarrel. Then a long way is left before you are mine. Yes, I'm jealous. Jealous so it hurts in my teeth, my teeth turn soft in my mouth of jealous.

When you say that the love for the two H's already disappeared when I was in Atepmoc you are lying indeed, my love. To yourself and to me. I remember so clearly myself asking: When did the lovestory with Hannelore end? And you answered, very fast and with a sharp sidelong look: Who says it is end? I remember that. One remembers when the whip gibes.

But I will not (do not dare) to say something about Hannelore and about what I feel in my bones.—Your memories of us are too full of "unreliablenesses" but mostly more true than the reality. But reality stands in no need to be true to life, so says Monsieur Boileau.

That I must type my envelopes shock me directly. If you told Coppera about me then she must know that I'm writing to you? Shall I put on a false name too? I have the adress of Martin from a wrong adressed envelope, preserve it because I know you are fond of him in a special way, a voluntary way. It would actually amuse me to be Martin Lindermann (*en route to l'Espagne*) and then—in out-folded state—Elin again. Like a real fold-out-girl as from a pornographic magazine. A picture only for your pleasure, a code which only you know the solution.

If I'm your breath then you are the very mystery behind the breath, you hit me in the middle, fling everything else overboard. I see terrified and delighted the fine trousseau (embrodered with the wrong initials) float on the sea ("The Rough") for a moment and then go down. Disappeared. After real manner of women I think that this anyway was made by fine linen, could be remade for other purpose ... But you laugh—a bit satanic quite frankly—against me with the remains of me between your teeth and my objection blows out of my mouth.

With what arrogance you ignore my laborious collected

trousseau. Indeed you make me naked. Don't you fear at all my fury that day the love is worn out? I wrote something four weeks ago after reading 30 pages in Rørvig of Böll's *Ansichten eines Clowns* and your stories, indeed, often give me the same kind of thoughts. Try to translate it here (it was actually written for you,—as everything I think):

So many stories is about "the lust of the flesh and the irreparable loneliness of the souls." (You barely know the quotation, it's from a swedish female-poet from about 1900. Now it is only quoted with becoming ironical distance). So many stories are songs about men's loneliness, men's search for that picture of love which are only given by glimpses. I'm thinking of all the stories (suddenly it seems to me that I never red anything else) about men's effort, their enormous effort in order to give women gifts, to give them their world, builted up through the years of reading and sensations and meditation and coined in stories told in bed in Atepmoc or in a tower in Heidelberg or in a field in Ireland. All this you give away for a kiss.

But when a woman reads these stories she reads them in another direction, sees another message, too, she sees your presents (so tempting in their tenderness and beauty) as demands. This gifts demand her "obliteration," she must follow the man in his world, let her be drowned in presents, follow the man in his dreams, make his dreams alive, turn herself into a dream. And she knows, she expects—from the very first moment in a new love-meeting—your anger and disappointment that day you see that your gifts isn't received in that spirit they were given. She knows your disappointment, turned into contempt in order to be bearable for yourself: Women are stupid, greedy and self-asserting. Stupid because you, the men, have been thinking everything out, have created everything,—greedy when they are not happy by that they are given and self-asserting when they demand their own diffuse univers accepted as real (banned into litter and sex as we say in danish, meaning that the ilegitimate children of a king are ennobled).—I'm mourning; for the love (the creating) that cannot endure. After that follows the loneliness only useable for telling at that time when the love was there.

Towards the loneliness (the disappointment, the end) we are leaded so necessary as the community (the hope, the beginning). This cycle is by most women perceived as created by men, it is him "to blame," she want to continue the creating of love, prefer to stay in the beginning. A day she sees that his touch was casual, that his gifts are not for her, that the love cannot be thought without its cessation, she understands that the love was a lever for something else, something in himself, not her business, something usefull: a new present. From him. As he can give to whom he wish! Then the beloved woman turns into a un-loved woman: a fearfull sight, a fury, a witch or only a tormentor, an envious creature hacking with the rests of her love: the selfishness, the greedyness, the demands. She sees her contribution (the giving up herself) swallowed, devoured and rised again as *something else*, something outside her. And she is seized by a deadly hate against this giver who used everything, who used her out.

The next time she is offered the love of a man (his world) she first sees the shadows from her dead sisters corpses—and turns into a whore, a sufragette, or very lonely. (Or the most scandalous, the most "perverse" of all: A woman with the same purposes as a man—a woman excluded from love.)

All this my dear Fitzy, I feel in a very strong way in the meeting with you. With Steffen I had not this "problematic" (what a word), with him there was a kind of cease-fire, a conspiracy,. a looking-at-the-world-together. With you there is quite another kind of life. And I want to live, I think I want it so much that I will die for it. I love you. I have decided to love you. You made the decision irresistable.

I know you prefer letters with concrete contents: stories, descriptions (best erotical), you want to fill them out yourself yes, put colours on. I send you a new cart of Copenhagen with marks and hidden signs which you can follow with the nail of your finger like Job scrabed his wounds with a potsherd!

Marijke is not a bit like me, I'm sorry to say. She is all the family of Steffen. I am not talking always, I'm talking in showers. I like to have letters to my homeaddress. It was not me waiting for hours on the steps, it was the letter. I meant I was funny. I haven't the slightest idea of what the postman looks like. I'm waiting everywhere. And not for hours but always. I remember myself standing on the floor in your bedroom, trying to explain you something. I could not and took a pair of dancing-steps in order to show you what I meant. I remember how much it pleased you, this simplicity and joy we had together.

To have few words demands clearness in mind. To have many words demands clearness in heart. You easy grows wild. It struck me that in a foreign language you cannot hear if your words are ridigiously, you can only hear your own thoughts.

I've never met such a absence of barriers from a man before. You must have made your women mad of love when you have been like that to them, too. My *Knepp* was good, very impersonal, I was thinking of nobody, so natural as washing oneself, a ritual, childish nearly. I fucked with the chap twice, it was the bitterness, the bitter need he took. Then I stopped because he approached to me, approached *your* regions. Do you understand? The fucking only helped me for a very short time. I put on the amulet again immediately of course. How can you think I didn't? I only took it off because of delicate reasons.

I meet you in another way than in my former erotic conceptions: lesser touch, more imagination. I tell you Fitzy, I imagine you so you would die from it if you were here. I feel you, you are with me, you are in me, you are alive in me (slowly and fast) and you die in me, you are flinged up in me, inside me and you stay there and get peace. I tell you, few have been so passionate faithfull to you as I in this months.

And I ... I catch a sweetness so unbearable that I disappear to myself, I dissolve, the top flies off, the bottom out. On Bornholm I found myself on the bed (an afternoon I stealed—stold?—me into my room) laughing against the roof and with my face wet by tears.

It is this I don't dare on the beatch because even the smallest help-from-hand is excluded and any other signs from body. The feeling of love (or the lechery) comes in waves. From the floating/flowing standstills the resevoir is filled slowly, the first power from the first wave kept, the next added. Addition. Addition untill no more addition is possible.

If I permit you to place me with maximum charm (what a

hidden phrase) in the hidden centre of your novel, I permit you everything. And I think you will love most of it. Maybe all. I permit you everything.

Elin

Letter 17
(Handwritten)

29th July 1975
Nørre Søgade

My dearest Fitzy,

Yes, my flat faces the lakes. Marijke and I went down there tonight, just across the Nørre Søgade. She has bread for the ducks and a letter in a bottle. The time is near to 9:00, the darkness is coming but the lake is still coloured, the air is misty (hazy?) by heat and smoke,—a bird, I don't know which one, flies by in quiet hurry, the strokes from wings are regular as morse-signals.

I'm happy tonight, have this 20 minutes together with you. Here are not much people, some few bourgeoises with dogs and a group of children. The five shout after the sixth: "Suckling, suckling!" Marijke is upset. An old man pass by, stiffly and regular as when you are walking with ski, and draws a invisible and absolute straight line after him. He wears a white linen-coat, wide trousers and new-chalked shoes. His complexion is sickly and sunburned. He reminds me of an asiat. I follow him with the eyes, turn the head and talk with Marijke—about the five which tease the one. Then I look after the old man again. He is still walking, but on the same spot as before. My reason tells me that he has stand still in the meantime, but if somebody looked sharp on me and said: "This is not a man but a sign on a chinese cardemono", I would say: "Yes, of course."

(Unsigned)

Goatshed
Atepmoc
España
30th July 75

Dearest Elin,

I have your long letter, photographs and presents, wear belt, light candle in your candle-stick of 1830, marvel at the fine material (wrapping the candle-stick), I like them all.

Your piece on men and women is very fine, although I do not think the Women's Liberation movement would approve.

You are right about Galway. Bethought me of an alternative: cottage in Wicklow near Laragh, pub run by ex-boxer (English), pool (Soldiers' Hole) in a narrow brown river, walks in low hills, undulating, weeds head-high. If it's vacant, we could be alone there. Have been looking at an atlas. Shetland Island too cold, near Arctic Circle. Channel Islands? Isle of Wight? Old Ross, given to floccinaucinihili-pilification, knows it, declares it impossible through summer. Frisian Islands? Amsterdam? Trying to get address of sculptor I know there, ex-Dublin. A city I like, have publisher there.

Wrong about me as "famous" writer: only poor pen-pusher in what Martin calls the word-whipping business, who cannot earn a living at it. Wrong about love-filled past, hot beds of youth, etc., compatability. More like ebb and flow of an endless struggle, opposing interests, and now mutual exhaustion, which sons add their burden to. My lost youth, a bit late, begins and ends with you. Wrong about Hannel too. Pastor in truth a dull fellow; she left him because she was better, more troubled, knocking about; whereas he craves peace and regular meals, the old in-and-out, dullness of settled life.

Shock to read of your *Knepp*. Was it the dry I CHING fellow? Hard to hear you gave yourself to another, who took what you gave, as though we were all the same (I and the multitude, I mean). I forgive you, but don't tell me if it happens again. All that wrecked here. Quarrels with Coppera surely bring me closer to you, not farther away? All touch boring when mechanical, losing what you call the bitterness, replaced by no sweetness, which only you can give, I regret to say, because I forsee difficulties ahead. But you are my life.

Your letter alarmed me a little: all that rush and glow. When you write of your youth past I must smile again, smile at you just turned 33 to my 48 years, thin in hope and lacking energy. But you declare—proudly—that you have enough strength for us both. And I believe you have. Away from you, mine goes, both hope and strength.

From the photos I see how much the short time in Bornholm gave you, just out of the sea, *Schöne Nixe*, but who takes the photos? The dry chap? Is there a lecher concealed somewhere in the dunes? Let's keep these jokes to ourselves.

My "regions", as you are pleased to call them! How much space have you in your body for my regions? I have just space enough for yours. The rest tires me, all that smut and glow. To have found you so late both delights and frightens me, because I feel like giving up everything just to be with you, feasting. All of you other than the strictly erotic, which you say I ignore, I do not ignore: it's your dance-steps in lieu of words, and you in the letters, such tearing of hair, all that I saw in your face and recognized at once: Elin = Trouble. And life, which I have so little of. And delight, which has flown out of the window because I am away from you. So there, my dear.

Heat continues. The water in the tank is soon used up and the place is not *fresh*, a very strong word with you as I seem to recollect. The Mediterranean offers up its high-summer smells: dead fish, tampons and Spanish Stomach. I do not walk. My son Nico works for Larry Rivers whom you never met: they are engaged in plaster and cement work for La Lunn's finca where you have never been. Miss Mouse mutters about leaving this futile existence for nursing in England. She is 37. Ex-Bunny Girl.

Hardly ever set foot in the Espejo Bar. Work while I can, squat on the terrace drinking corriente wine and casera, regard the village below. Coppera entertained until 3:00 am with Wittgenstein, that laughing jackass in his tall house. I tell her that we must part company. She agrees. Address your envelopes as you please. She regards them as bombs. And so they are.

I cannot say I miss you, because your living touch has shrivelled up in me, and you must touch again to bring me back to life again. It's almost August, the month when the animals stifle in the hellpits, birds die in their cages. In five weeks I'll be leaving for filthy London.

The three lads tried to get to Nerja on ONE bicycle, fell at the first corner when a car came around. The middle one has 4 stitches in his knee. They spend much time indoors, writing Conan Doyle-type stories, quarreling at table, running errands, listening to the bitching which continues between their parents, not edifying, and must continue until nothing remains but gnawed bones. It's not pleasant for them. But as you point out, kids are selfish, have their own protection devices. Ours are spoilt.

Insects teem here in the great heat, proliferating, Terral blowing hot air from the mountains teeming with vipers, spiders weaving their webs, knock them down and they're back next morning, armies of ants banqueting on dead flies. Dispatch one fly and another stands on its corpse: mourning or having a closer look or eating its brother? One darts off with a mortally injured companion: can one assign kind motives? They eat you alive on the terrace, where I feel like a cadaver already, naked from the waist up and covered in them. Brown corduroys seem to hold a fatal attraction, with scores slaughtered by a whisk. Do they see connections between brownness and dung? If so they err, for I shower regularly, under drips.

Stout Raffo ("El Cebolla," the Onion, as his father before him, and *his* father before him, Raffo the bachelor perhaps the last of a long imperishable line of Onions) works like blazes in the bar, roaring out the orders; but by siesta time is discovered sleeping with arms across a chair, or in a stunned state behind the bar-counter, the heavy exhausted face resting on the palm of the hand, the milky blue eyes fixed on some far remote point beyond the open door. Or—a bold alternative—the right hand convulsively clutching the crown of the head as though the brains within were boiling. He wears monkish sandals over brown silk socks, a stylish detail, manages the great coffee-machine. His feet are killing him.

Fellow of 39 buried today, the poet brother of Placido

72

Espejo, old women weeping, Placido weeping. In an effort to breathe, we have knocked down the wall to left of front door and knocked out former door into cellar, then another door (fit for pigmies) into patio where shrunken vine hangs gasping. With egress from kitchen now possible, light floods in from another quarter, and air too, when it moves. We sleep on the roof, Coppera and I, not well. Not well, the planet Venus winking brightly in a mauve sky turning indigo. Three conjunctions, no less, occured between the planets Saturn and Jupiter in 7 BC. Triple conjunctions only occur every 139 years. In the case of the constellation Pisces, which is linked astrologically with Israel and hence with the Jewish people, this only happens every 99 years.

Half a bottle of raw cognac a day is not good for the nerves. Red wine stains the teeth but brush well in a circular fashion with dry bicarbonate of soda on your toothbrush and all will be well. Eggs make one caustic; too many eggs consumed produces colesteral (spell). Larry Rivers swears by the Atepmoc Egg: note the orange yolk of free-ranging hens, no battery-breds here. All is design: the patterns the house-flies make, the haphazard arrangement of dead ones on the terrace, the vine leaves in the patio arranged by chance (the wind), the kahl-burner's neat woodpile. The cattle on the edge of the dump above the long cattle-shed. It would not surprise me greatly to see the heads of llamas or gnus poking through the windows, or to encounter a dromedary on the path. These cows do not behave like cows, lolling around the ravine, apparently constipated, compared to Irish cattle—Ballina awash in cowshit. Nature lies always under God's protecting hand, and Satan has no final say there. A spider tired of weaving webs.

Write me more of your fierce letters. They are my fixes, my powerful injections. With your next, sellotape in some hair from your head, from under your arms, from between your legs—seeing you refuse to send me "unfresh" photo of you naked on your bed. Women used to favour Byron so, sort of testamonials. If I cannot have you all in one piece, mail me bits of you. *Du.*

Dreams. Taking-you-away-with-me dreams. Eating you dreams, first your ears, then your toes, take it easy, work steadily up, your hips, sex, heart. Forgive me my greed my dear, I am too greedy for what I want. Go on calling me your beloved and I believe we will have it. There will be no silence or any awkwardness after these torrid letters. You are strolling out of Cataluña in your black poncho, the man-in-the-lift is leering at you from the door, the stone-cutters at the corner are calling to you. We are drinking gin in Café Español. Now you are dressed in a russet coloured woolen Phrygian cap. We undress so quickly this time. The *Kuss* never ends, dragging your heart out by the roots. We go out again. We are ravenous now. You stand in the doorway of the Buñuel Bar drinking white wine in "the depths of the sea" oh!

> Schöne Nixe, im Schleirgewand
> Ensteigen der Meerestiefe

The hotel bedroom with lights out is undersea (although four floors up). We drink the white wine. We are naked as fishes. We have *fischgrütigen Zähnen*. We fall on each other. Tearing each other to bits.

Had a dream lately of someone naked bleeding from making hot love as if scourged. I had another attack, this time on the terrace. It seemed my back was torn open, I was a gutted fish, the churchbell was beating me with its heavy strokes. Forgive me, dearest Elin, I could be so gentle. Being without you makes me ravenous.

Fitzy

CHAPTER 8: Letters 19, 20, 21, 22, 23

The Spellbound Child Grown Old

Letter 19

12th august 1975
Copenhagen

Dearest,

Just have your letter, mailed the 6th august from Atepmoc. Do not shrivel up now, I am at you in a couple of weeks, in "filthy" London, in any flat at all, doesn't matter, the place will be piculiar because we are together.

So much you hurt me by saying:—"As though we were all the same." I forgive you that sentence. I will not write more about this case, you will read it in a wrong way, a way which make you more suffering. And answer me in a way which make me more suffering. I only want to kiss you, to touch you, to see my dreams in you as in a mirrow, to see mine continue in you and *yours* continue. Do not shrivel up. When you read this lines there is maybe only twenty days left until we are sleeping together again. *Mein lieber Liebling.* You letters always make me happy, now I'm crying, not for my own sake, but only for you. No, for myself too. If you are shrivelled up in the meantime, what then can I do. Do not say London is no good for you because when you leave Spain it means that you can see me again, kiss me again, *wieder, wieder kneppen mit mich.*

Believe in my calm from Bornholm. Believe in my new name, believe that Bornholm is full of promises. I will protect you and you me. I will give you life, you will give me rest. If you cannot live in London I can find a place for you in Denmark so that we can touch each other frequently. It has been in my mind for a long time but I will not say anything about it. It was in my mind already the last days in Atepmoc because I knew so well what you meant to me. Is it this you call my rush?

I don't want to rush you, least of all, I want you to follow yourself which I hope (what word is greater than HOPE??)

will mean to follow together with me. It was what I said at the Malaga-dinner, the lovely one, when I praised you because of your refusing of being "normalized" your refusing of following anything but yourself. I didn't tell you anything about my fear, my inside weeping, from the fear that this could mean excluding me. I don't want to rush you. I want to love if you want me to. But Denmark is a dangerous country, you can find no vision of freedom here. The Danes have used up their dreams of power, at least on a national scale. All Scandinavians of course believe in a well-run world, I don't: the mean things are just as strong as the fine things. Everything in nature is dangerous to a Dane: LIVSFARE JORDSKRED (Unsteady Earth) the sign says near Dr Rasmussen's house by Thulevej. But all Thule Expeditions over ice and snow are ended and Rasmussen is dead. The window of his hidden house is an eye that looks over Kattegat. The modern Danes don't like air, close up all the train windows when they are travelling. So, no freedom here. Also that kept me back (keep) from this idea.

All loving persons promise each other that *their* life will be different. We are so old (I am old in a way—and very childish in another) that we can see the dangers, I think we can. It makes us unsure of course, so many ways are wrong ways, so many things you cannot do and still keep the essence, the loaded essence from the first meeting, the presentiment, the meetings on the highways in the dark nights ... I hardly know what I am writing, just put words down, do not use the dictionary, just talking to you, touching my breasts in between, I'm naked, alone at home, writing in the *bleu heur*, I will not put on my lamp because then I have to take the curtains before the window and it is so hot, Denmark is the hottest country in Europe for the time, 32-36 degrees, if you call it that (something about Fahrenheit and Celsius I cannot remember). Very hot, anyway. And very dark now. I go for a while, put on the lamp and curtain and make me some food.

Now my pictures mingle in each other. I've had such a dull childhood. Always I was bored, deeply *bored*. When was my game coming out? All this demi-waiting that reduced my life to nothing. Begins to say already the lies of authority and power that came later.

You use often the word "strolling" about me. It pulls inside me of ... so many things, pleasant and unpleasant, presentiments I don't know about, I don't know if it is true or untrue. Am I a strolling person? Or do you want me to be a strolling person (meaning: so you can leave me with fresh heart)? It reminds me of a certain Fraulein Klein. My handwriting is different from hers. The sentence "her last abuse" got my hairs on end for eagerness to understand what is said there. I love those shortstories so much. Do you know them? Were there stronger reasons to write these stories than the langsam novel, which is in an odd way not quite true? Well, to me. Does he really believe that he can avoid the guilt by only describing "real" persons' abuse of each other. If that is too suspect to you then throw the typewriter out the window.

(Unsigned)

I will stop for this time. Put also a epistle from weeks ago about the lakes outside my windows. I'm still naked, wear only your amulet, my dear. Want to say you everything, to let you touch me everywhere and to touch you. To kiss your sex. So much I loved that. And your mouth and your sex again. To bring the taste from your sex together in our mouths. I loved that. To whisper in your mouth with no words. You *must* miss me. You must not shrivel up.

(Unsigned)

Letter 20

17th of August 1975
Sunday, Copenhagen.

My beloved,
You wrote: "which only you can give me, I regret to say, because I see difficulties ahead." Surely they are there, but what kind of difficulties do you see? Or do you put the word difficulties instead of disappointments? Be brave my love, even the disappointments we will laugh at, laugh Mr Disappointment up his face, fling it back to him and not to each other. We will trick him.

Now I tell you something which maybe sound strange to your ears, which you maybe misunderstand as you misunderstood "my Knepp": On Bornholm I gave you up. Meaning: If I am

77

your woman, if we are for each other, then we are, and only work is ahead. If not, then I go on searching (my search started with you), weeping of course but not complaining, not confused any longer. No.

In order to calm you: this serious, desterny-heavy words are only substitutes. In real life I am mostly joy and lovefull, taking dancingsteps in lieu of words. My letters are monologues below the actions, my life is dialogues, action. Remember that you was able to make me happy, easy, clear. And I did so to you. The others perceived you as sombre, intellectual, fierce. To me you was cheerfull. And gentle, gentle and deep. Yes you gave me abandonment. Drinking water at the spring at the flowering-abletree-place on the way to the Third River. You are tender my Fitz and cheerfull. We was laughing so often. Have you forgotten that?

Elin

Letter 21
(never received)

Goatshed, Atepmoc, España
Monday evening
18 August 75

Dearest Elin—
Been feeling most disturbed and unsettled, fearing my letter—delayed in the sending—had never reached you, wanted to phone you, felt at a loss, felt you slipping away to some unrecognizable place, making me feel even worse, quite helpless, no hope of you ever writing back, or if you did the letter would be lost; or, if it came, it would have the wrong sort of contents. But that's only Old Despair's brother with his endless lies, for your letter did come, held over a weekend when I wasn't here and left under basket of stuff, and your voice speaking through the tapping machine calmed me, put away all the fears (of losing you), confirming your wildness (head hair, body hair) and beauty, and I was no longer lost and became calm again.

And always and ever you surprise me: the colour of your hair, the length of it, the swathe you send me, even to the way you cut it. I felt nostalgic for your body, to be with you again, in you

78

again, making me wild but also calming. How strange your colouring: long brown hair, green eyes. And at times, both bored and upset in company, I feel your belt bite into me, and I am calm again. More than that: excitement and life begin to run again. Your below-hair, I nose it, bite it, from far away some of your spices drift to me: your Wild Musk Oil described offhandedly as "a prehistoric perfume," my sweetest one.

Your presents here are my talismen protecting me from the demons (fucker Knud Andersen fucking you in the wooden house in the Swedish forest), the 1830 pewter candlestick in the window embrasure, your long piece of cloth (which I like very much) hung over the bed (where nothing happens anymore), over the djalabo. How purposeful the way you drifted towards me. And when you say: 20 days, London, flat, bed, touching you again, it's right, and above all what I wanted to hear. And when you say "*Wieder, wieder kneppen mit mich*," how calming that "*mich*" is. And everything begins to flow again, and I in it, pulled towards you, longing for you, entangled in that long strange coloured hair, your calmness (hid in wildness), your slanty green eyes, your mouth that is my fruit, the nights with you that are my hope, my only hope. And I think: all will be right again.

I have your hair out on my desk. It's alive. I washed it. Washed you. Turned you over, cleaned you. You let me, you were not ashamed, the bedroom was a stable, you were a mare being groomed, I was your loving groom. You are down among the wild roses in Little Russia. You take me there. You reveal to me those unpeopled beaches, a threemaster in the haze, a swan flying over.

You are even right about my *Werke*—the early stuff was the best. I had the excitement then, writing it in Singapore, working with excitement, and it's come back to me.

Your letters always make *me* happy. They come out of nowhere, strike into me. I spent a boozy time in Nerja. You weren't there, dancing behind a pillar with a glass of Bloody Mary in one hand, humming to yourself, jealous of Suzanne, that bitch in the tight slacks. You were dancing there, humsing, in a wicked mood. I watched you. I went up to you. You cursed me. It was your 33rd birthday. We couldn't eat the rabbit in Jesú's place. Slept back to back that night, no touch, no

Kneppen, you had thrown your boots into the room. Was it a bad night? No, it wasn't.

My telephone number in London is 734-7200. I leave here on I think 3rd September, reach London 6th or 7th. School begins on 8th, Monday. When could you come? How long can you stay? We need to be together, dearest. These letters are catching fire. We need the touch again. Come soon, come soon.

Too dark to continue now. I end here. It's Monday. Soon I will see you. It will be another Monday. This halflife will end. You will end it with me. How I long for that, *Schwesterlein*!

All my love always. I feel calm again.

Fitzy

Letter 22 (never received)

Goatshed, Atepmoc, España
21 August 75

Dearest Elin,
My uncalm is you, the goodness so near, I have just to reach out.

Your Sunday letter came hard on the heels of yours of Copenhagen August 12, your hair that binds me, your photo eyes that regard me, lift me up out of this pit of uncertainty that I am drowning in.

Observe me, please, rigid as a wooden figure lying in a sacarium, the noble brow corrugated, the nose thin as a pen. The sound of a mule indicates, at long last, Monday. It's Monday morning. But wrong again. The churchbell strikes four times to indicate position on the dial, then seven measured strokes for the time: it's seven o'clock on Sunday evening. I fell exhausted into bed at 1:15 pm. Mnemogne: mnemonic (I love that word: Mnemonic) aids to exploration of sequence and event (as in the work of Conrad). The spellbound child grown old. Dying of indolence and excessive expectancy. I saw an image with multiple forms quiverring in the light.

When you wrote: "On Bornholm I gave you up," it was a deadly blow. But soon the reprieve: "*If* I am your woman, if we are for each other"—it puts all right again, it's like a pact. I know you found me. I know I found you. We are thus, to others different. Let us hold onto each other, never let go. London, even, is transformed: you have transformed it. When you assure me that soon we will be sleeping together, I feel so happy. There are woods around, not too far away up the hill. Crouch End Playing Fields, we can take beer and sandwiches, watch the cricket, a very strange near-static game played by chaps in white, English ghosts, demanding loudly: "How's ZATTT??" Queens Wood is always deserted (the Plague dead were buried there), Hampstead Heath is fine, all horizons, copper beeches. To be with you there, what better. Take a taxi from the BEA terminal. Stay above ground.

I was going to write to you again, when your Sunday letter came, again our thinking the same. Touching you was like that, satiation impossible, you come and go, waxing and waning, I can never have enough of you, never exhaust my pleasure in you, you refresh me, I come alive again.

If you object to "strolling," then perhaps "prowling" might be closer the mark. You coming up from the little Plaza, how quick you were to see the door ajar. I have only to make a small gesture, you'd see it in the dark. How good if the shaking continues in London. Already it begins a little now. I have no calming Bornholm (full of promises) to adjust me, just moons like suns at night, dogs like devils barking as if pleading, and me turning and turning as if on a spit.

The other night at Larry Rivers' place, at a dinnerparty, Pernille arrived late, witty lady not too sober soon, brought up your name (Coppera was present, making up to a water-ski chap), and the room collapsed around me, the people in it disappeared, I had to go home, could not say another word .... It was as if you had touched me or brushed up against me, your name invoked in the room, where nothing interests me. So much for calmness.

Fitzy

III

Copenhagen, London, Connemara,
Berlin, Naxos,
Upper Washington State (US)

CHAPTER 9: Letters 24, 25, 26, 27, 28

The Oppersite Land

Letter 24

Copenhagen,
monday night
the 29. september 1975

My dearest,

Home again, not too bad. The journey back from London was awfull, the flight delayed for two hours, sitting there with "fasten your seatbelts and no smoking" and more and more hungry and thirsty, no money for a beer, the temptation for a beer anyway. But very wise I was, took no beer and luck for that because home in Copenhagen I phoned everybody and nobody was at home. 8 o'clock my ex-mother in law answered the phone saying: Steffen has just given up waiting for you, has been waiting together with Marijke all afternoon in his favourite pub, playing billiard. Then family-meeting at ex-mother with snaps, beer and food and little Marijke. I was surprisingly happy.

Sunday morning hard for me. I was going to phone you 10 o'clock but didn't. You must not disturb my normal-life any longer, no bad winter like the bad summer I've had, only happiness when we see each other.

I've been very active, cleaning up the house, walkings with Marijke and her girlfriend Ingeborg, collecting chestnuts along the lakes, it was sun and storm yesterday. Phoned today, asking for studio-time, have had a tape waiting all summer for cutting, no energy for doing it, but now I have and got the cut-time immediately. Good. Planning a dinnerparty yesterday evening together with Sweet-Anna, started to invite people today. Good.

Steffen find my text about MIN BY rather bad as you did, rhetorical. Very pleasant to talk to him after this two weeks of 'oppersite' life with you. My strict poet, my moistful beloved. Kissing your sex while you were sitting on me: I felt crucified. I never did exactly that before. The need for you will come again, it will return, the desperate need for you, I try to push it in front of me, meeting it when I meet you again.

Will go and sleep now, reading your Bildung first for a while. Tender regards to your kids (I often feel pity for children, is it without ground?), cheerfull regards for R and tell him I'm no golddigger. And love for you, my love.

Elin

Letter 25

Finsbury Park
6th October 75

Queens-Wood-walker, bad au pair girl, disturber of drain-diggers, green-eyed I Ching questioner, lover of evening skies, traveller-for-short-ditances-in-London-taxis, writer-by-windows, lover of back-scratching, rearranger of furniture, moistful mistress, warmth-in-bed ... I miss you.

A week has gone by and the flowers and stuff we gathered are dead, thrown out. Have washed your dressinggown and was all set to post it when I found these underthings of yours. Will post them with the dressinggown which you are probably in need of.

Walked across Hampstead Heath by night last weekend, after pointless drinking with Silly de Warr until 4:00 am in an all-night American Steak House. He has laid out £500 for film option. I missed you. The night sky was if anything more extraordinary than before. I went by Kenwood over padlocked gates, the huge 250-year-old beech tree, into Highgate Wood, scaling padlocked wooden gates with drunken ease, a shadow flitting, missing you all the time, the night and its illuminations would have delighted you, with no sinner about and *Knepp* in the leaves on, it wasn't cold. You were here, steaming up the bathroom, letting your coffee get cold—only a few hair clips about to remind me.

Send print of yourself seated in the red armchair, if it comes out. When is your dinnerparty? Pity for children—yes, I feel that sometimes. Weekend excitement for mine: Mario the tomcat (sometimes "Gooseberry") fought another cat. "Liquorice" caught a pigeon (the place swarms with them, parasites of the air). Russel Boggis (a bad boy) fell off a motorbike. Paul half strangled Ben with the clothesline. Tier-up claimed the-tied-up-one liked it. They live in a fast dream.

Would we live well together? I like your working habits, your making-comfortable habits, moving stuff around, correcting errors, you'd correct errors in me. We will have to create our own country: the "Oppersite Land". Now a very respectable black Paterfamilias walking with sons (presumably) jigging along, wagging heads, followed by four dark girls crouched under one umbrella, bound for the Tube, the place where we came in by, set off from, how many *Kussen mit Kneppen* in between? Old woman sitting in cement shelter, heavy traffic passing, nothing to see but cement, traffic, dirty air, funeral bushes—that ground-down life.

I wake early, after six, after supper fall asleep before the fire, wake up at 1:00 am, stagger to bed, too feeble even to miss you—or that "other savage thing": a woman's embrace (Pavese). He likely feared women, had ejaculatio praecox, which can be cured by any understanding sympathetic lady, none of whom Pavese encountered, looking for his Cross. Women probably sensed the search for misfortune and kept off.

So, so, so. My dearest. Write. Keep in touch. Your touches I miss. Here a poor touch through the post. Better than nothing.

Fitzy

Letter 26
(Handwritten, no address)

14th October

Still looking for the right dictionary. I would like very much to give you that: an outline of our lovelanguage, the oppersite language, with secret meaning hidden in the appearance. Like the wise-men-middle-age-language (*Rosen-Kreuz-Brüder-Ordnung*): I feel our love more and more exclusive, belonging to very few points,—no, I don't think we could live steadily together. But I miss you, I don't give you up, we will make love together again. Soon I hope.

My dinnerparty took place last friday. Successfull, people say. I felt a little strange, too many people, too many I didn't understand why was in my room. Kissed in despair (because I'm in love with you) a person who kissed me in despair (because he is in love with my girlfriend) who is in love with Thorkild who is in despair of unknown person. All very painfull and superficial and disillusionate and childish. Steffen was not there. Steffen hates this stuff—is rather hating for the time, contempting as usual. Marijke enter more and more her own world. It is good. She said yesterday: "It doesn't matter you have Fitzy as a fiancé but don't marry him—then you will let Steffen down." And I remember the sign of you drying the hair of Ben on the floor in the frontroom.

I think I will stop—is rather depressed. Send paper and color-pencil and other stuff for the kids as soon as I get time.—Think of next summer my love.

Elin

Letter 27
(Handwritten)

Sunday 25. oct. 75

My dearest Fitzy my strange lover.
I can only tell you sadness today. I'm heavy like mire. Your punishment of sending no letter is effectfull. I'm suffering. I'm sitting at my window, reading your Bildung all day. All the days which means all the nights. What a study in beauty and melancholy. The description of the death of your mother is unforgettable. And so is many other pieces, too. You as a child listening at the party going on, unable to sleep. Very beautifull—your language is most beautifull, so powerfull and slowly like waves—sensations so sharp received and remembered. The love stuff moves my heart to the throat—so jealous I'm, so much I recognize you, so filled with melancholy I am when I read it. As you were when you wrote it I suppose. As you are, my love.

I'm sick again for longing for you. All over again. Wasting time, looking at a nail on the wall, thinking of you, of us.

I was out drinking last night. With good old Steffen. He asked me to go home with him. I said no; preferred to go home to nobody as I must in this months (going on and on) because I cannot go home to anybody but to you (a book. Yours. which pains me). "It is difficult to let a beautifull girl go home alone" Steffen said while I waved at him down the dark rainy street.

Now he found me beautifull. Now he is suffering. And I can do nothing. Not even enjoy that revenge I have wanted for years. The rules are indeed cruel. I will never be able to forget you. Once more. Am longing for you, reading about your dreams, writing against your dreams. Again I'm longing for you. Too much. Send me a letter about us.

I kiss you.
Elin.

(When Coppera return? I would be more calm for you and the kids when she is home again. Cannot send stuff for the kids. Would cost 4£.)

Letter 28

Finsbury Park
October ending 75

My dearest,
Sorry for silence. Wanted to phone you a few times, writing seemed ineffective. Have your white nightdress half-packed with I believe your underthings but put off posting them, and yesterday came the belt and a little note.

I have to see you.

I sometimes hear your voice, repeating a single word, once in a wood, perhaps saying my name. I think it must be my way of loving you: hearing your voice when you in fact are not there. Wish I could get out of the mess I am trapped in, making feeble efforts towards that end. Hopefully København after Xmas. Cannot think of going to bed with you, most moistful, that time seems far away now.

Tobin the Umbrian with his Belgian light-of-love are here now, I have given up the main bedroom and sleep in the front room. She fills the bedroom with unguents, he grouses, tipples on Ramrods. A silent couple somehow unquiet. The Berlin

Martin's mother died, only 58, destroyed by big operation on brain. He has moved to old Moabit, with a young girl from Cologne, aged 16, is translating Murdoch novel for some publisher, asks when I return to Berlin. I wonder also.

Feeling very unsettled, disturbed even, needing you. One letter says Greece, another says Atepmoc. Would not be unduly put out if I never saw latter place again, wishing for a place where we would not be known, hardly seen, so that I could have you in peace. But is that possible?

I felt you would be hurt a little when I was drying Ben's hair, excluded somehow, which I did not wish. Marijke's remark about me—us, Steffen—hit me too. I feel sorry for Steffen, it must have been painful for him when you turned away from him.

Attraction is only possible, seemingly, when one is not entirely oneself. I try to remember you here, the Tube train ride of 25 stations, our arrival here in the rain, you in the front room, starving kisses. Then you and your kisses disappear. And I disappear too.

The *Kuss*: the horse rearing when the shadow falls.

Ladies with faces that are not your face abound, speaking in various accents of matters that do not interest me. You have a special lingo to reach me, reach into me; you use it, shaking your head, this won't do at all.

The Umbrian's moll uses much scent, the cushions I sleep on stink of it, I don't like it, you never used scent except that prehistoric essence of moose. I miss you marching around, moving very proud for a tall girl, ship in full sail. The lads now and then inquire of Elin. I tell them "Copenhagen".

Sometimes I see the stout mad girl worrying an old man in the cement shelter down the way. She never stops moving, the fidgets of the insane, pulling at him like a child or pup. Father (presumably) ashamed to take her hand, so she puts it into his pocket anyway, going home for lunch, or to the betting-shop. Soon they are back, she pestering the old man who now threatens her with his raised stick.

Here they come again.

Fog clearing up, cold enters the flat, Paul gone out with his new big sketchbook. Will close here, reduced to mumbles, dribble, *nada*.

Fitzy

CHAPTER 10: Letters 29, 30, 31, 32, 33, 34

Little Caves of Opposite Life

Letter 29
(Handwritten and undated)

Wednesday

My dear

Have just received your letter. Your signature is nearly disappeared, only a strange line is left—indeed you have no good time. You miss. And your miss is old, you have missed many things for a long time. I don't think I can cure you, but maybe I can make the things a little sweeter for you—put sugar on the pills, that bitter medicine you have to swallow every day and which you don't want to share with anyone. I noticed that very much in London: You can give (and take) but you cannot share. Or you don't want (with me anyway).

I miss your touch, I miss your kiss, I miss our *besonderes Kuss*. I'm looking forward to see you again and kiss again. I hope very much it will be after Christmas because I have to see you frequently now because I deny myself to think of you always. As I did this summer.

Could we live together for some months in Atepmoc next summer? Or Greece. Strange that you have avoid Greece. The only country which maybe could cure your melancholy (and not only ignore it like Spain does).

(Unsigned)

Letter 30

12.11.75

Hello

This instead of phoning you. I have a feeling that Coppera is at home. I have been unable to write to you in the time being. Whatever I put down on paper I felt it would hurt you, harm you. I am in a kind of prison, and I see you very much in a kind of prison, too. I don't mean "the mess you are trapped in," but I see you very much in your own prison, your own prejudices, which—of course—create "the mess".

This letter is an attempt for me to break out of the prison and I ask for your help. I am asking for trouble ... Please, my dear, if you love me a little still, please write me a fearsome and cruel and brave letter about us. About what is dream and what is reality, about your disappointment (I know my own) and please, give up the hope that I am stupid ...

I am asking very serious for this. If you refuse I am afraid I start hating you, no—contemning you. Try to write to ME, not to your dream-picture of me. Tell me in your own words (as the teacher said when one should re-tell a piece of literatur) how it is with us. I have deceived you in a way, let you build up an image of me which is not real. And you have kept it, turning your back on me when I tried to touch it, giving me silence, grimaces and quotations ...

Please, my beloved let us save our dream by naming the reality, let us say awfull things so the rest can be true. The ghosts grow and grow when you never face them. You should know that ...

Yours
Elin

Letter 31

London
15th November 75

Hello Yourself,
Your *Cri de coeur* of 12th November arrived this morning. This weak ribbon is not the only weak thing today. Fog for two or three days only clearing now, on miserable damp winter scene, and this but the beginning.

My wife is here. I sleep alone, cook my own scraps. Am sorry I could not speak to you on the phone. You sounded sad, rather beaten. Poor you. Poor everybody. I, being stupid, do not understand what you ask of me in your short letter, what you want (wish) of me—nor did I see what line you would have me ignore (forget), overlook, forgive. As to what's between us, I know only that I want to be with no one else, listen to no one else, eat with no one else, sleep with no one else, look at no one else, live with no one else.

As to dream (perhaps the only word we cannot put quotation marks around) and "reality", whatever that may be, well they are for me one and the same. Someone—I suspect Frisch—has wisely said that it's the secrets a man and a woman, a loving couple, keep from each other that makes them a pair. And I fancy that is true.

How or why do you want me to see you otherwise than as I see you, dreaming you? You, very sweetly, bring me to myself. You speak and write a very strange language that only I can understand. Do you want it otherwise? You want me to see you as hard, heavy-footed, obtuse, impatient with the jelly that is me, at times? You are hard, heavy-footed, obtuse, sometimes, mostly not. You are the best warmth I know. Other mouths, lips, to eat or kiss or just spit out stupidity and venom, are everywhere. You snore. Even your snoring charms me. I can turn you on your side. How do I really see you—what a question!

I find good in you, the only nutriment I know. Making love to you nourishes me. I tried it since with another here, total failure, I might just as well have gone to bed with a lynx, or a snake. I will not think of you, because I am numb with disappointments, am dull with disappointments, am half-man without you. The only "disappointment" I found, as you warned me, here, was your deafness to what I said sometimes, because I suppose you were thinking in Danish, heard only sounds. That didn't (doesn't) matter either. I cannot even recall the "happiness" of our being in bed together, whatever pulleys and levers were pulled in you and in me, by you for me, by me for you, or both together pulling for us both, the one; except that I know full well that you for your part were reaching deep into me, and I for my part deep into you. I remember the other day, after that bloody publisher left, closing the curtains, a moment with you there by the window, pulled towards you. The soldier-on-leave with his famished girl. Is that what you call "dreaming"?

Is this the answer you want from me? Probably not. Certainly I could imagine you hating me; even that would raise me up. Of our love again I cannot think, it's too much. Reach out and I fall. I reach out and you fall. This miserable time stops; a better time begins. I miss it.

I sleep spitefully, as if sick, alone. I don't want to return to Atepmoc, to all that evesdropping and gossip. You are right in what you say of ("my") Spain. Greece? Another lingo. I have no money. I wish we could work towards something, I mean for each other, I mean to join again. Some writer—Frisch again very likely—speaks of watching the woman getting into a bath, it means that and no more, another body occupied with washing itself, so that it can get out and dress and start wagging its tail again (MF of course would not express it as vulgarly). Love for the other body has gone, and the mystery has gone too. The adored shell becomes just another woman, one of millions, your mother, your sister. Dampness and stinks remain.

I had to fumigate the flat after that couple left. You are the cool lady who sees the snake in the bag and is not too alarmed. Or goes up in the lift with the lift-man who asks you if you are married, when the pair of us must reek of semen and salt-swoll'n cunt, of Honeymoon. Or down-faces the Atepmoc youths outside Fat Luis's Bar el Montes. You are that cool one. Cool, we must assume, because you are on your way, sailing towards me.

Alright, fair's fair, you invent me, too. I am not the *Brüderlein* you think I am. Out of thousands of possible *Schwesterleins* I invent only you. Of course I invent you. Why complain of that? Doesn't a child, who knows nothing, invent the whole world? *Si!*

Wish I could rise in the morning and make love to you as we did in Wandsworth, to the frank amazement of someone passing by outside: seeing a naked couple as all one piece like a flower in the jungle. How I miss all that "lewdness" and love. Not a drop since.

(Unsigned)

Letter 32
(Handwritten)

My dear love—
So foolish, in a way, to quarrel about what love is like ... I mean we are—you in one way, I in another way—in the middle of the love. And we will both change a bit, I guess.

Thank you for your letter. Of course I am glad for your letter. My heart you don't have to ask for. You have it still. Even behind a glass, and frame. Your poem is still by my bed and your picture still by my table. You look sombre at me. And strictly. I alternatively shock you and make you sad. Like Venteuil's daughter in the room with the girlfriend. Found this German dictionary for you some weeks ago. Hope you like it.

You have no money? You cannot come after Christmas? Then I will go for Bornholm after Christmas, thinking of you. I am not sorry either not to see Atepmoc again. It was a lovely place and a fantastic time, but I don't think I liked the people there so much. We will find out something. Jurij and wife may go for Crete, can have a free house there and a very large one.

I think I quit my steady job after Christmas. Have been in my mind for a long time now. Was going to tell you about it, when you saw a cat in a window ... And interrupt me.

About my deafness: Yes, in a way I had to think in Danish now and then—but more (rather) I have to think in "Elinish". And you have to think in "Fitzish". Our dictionary belongs to the flesh, my love.

Yes, you are here. And you are not here. So I miss you. So write. I have not many words myself for the time being.

Yours forever
Elin

Letter 33

My love
I miss you. It is very storming, my curtains are blowing in the room. I miss a letter from you. I miss you. I have put photo-pictures in a book tonight, my past. After April 75 I've got a heavier look in my face. Please come into my world, beloved. Talked with my old friend Volmer tonight, about the past. A past-night night. Please share with me, my beloved.

They have a party going on downstairs, cheap music, it is nice, they share their reality with me. Should have been in the theatre tonight with some people but phoned that I was ill and am in a way but not in the throat or the nose. I miss you. Don't give me up, it is too early, we must work more, love more before giving up each other my love. Bad you cannot come after Christmas, bad, bad.

Write a lot of poems for the time being, cannot see if they are good or bad, doubt all over. Cannot write prose, have no strength, no intelligence. I also remember that afternoon by the window, I was weak in my bone from love, we were well-bathed and well-fucked, a little food, much fire, some minutes when the dream and the reality met each other. Don't say I despise dreaming, read back in my old letters, I remember I wrote something like: "We are dreaming. The dream comes true if we are clever to dream. This is to believe in magic."

Sorry I couldn't hear your radio piece, more sorry I couldn't hear you giving interview, meaningfull or not—doesn't matter to me,—I don't understand english if you remember.

Read *Gantenbein* newly. It is an outstanding book, mar-velous, an absolut strange world to me, the love-stuff I mean. Can hardly recognize a bit of Lila in myself. Red also Borges, I admire him, read him with strucking heart but he is not healthy to me, I'm dropped down again in the terror from my youth I had enough (or not enough) of. This double/double/double-essens makes me not wiser but only lesser fit for survival.

Wrote a poem some days ago about being victim of jealousy, very sad, loving, bitter. Your sad loving bitter mistress miss you.

Monday afternoon

Have turned the half of your telephonenumber now four times and put back the phone again. *Please tell me when I best can call you.* Have Coppera a job how? I could call you in the daytimes from the phone here at DR. Or in nighttime from home,—don't matter. I miss you so much. Is it really impossible for you to come to Copenhagen in january or february? It is impossible for me to come to London because I keep on working steadily untill april 76.

Had a dream last night about somebody who gave us 1000£ if we could live in a cottage near the sea. You might easily call that a wish-dream. Do you believe in next summer? Believe that you will be able to rise money for some months together? It could be very cheap. I can rise money for myself (some) in one way or another way. I can take my last month-wage and run away and I can rent out my flat and have a little money in that way. But it will be difficult to me to save money for both for us—unless the dream from last night was clairvoyance ... Send this in a hurry because I miss you so much and because I send so few words the last couple of times, my Fitz.

(Unsigned)

Letter 34

15. dec. 1975

My beloved

I can not work today, I'll write to you, all day, since you cannot write to me. I'll talk, scatter as you say. I'm tired today, in a good way, heavy, slowly, my bike nearly stood still on the way out here, even if it is not blowing today. A pearl-grey morning with threatening sky, violet-violence, Blake. It is nice to scatter in another language, judgements excluded. As when I heard my Grandmother Lemm (means prick) singing old german psalmes, with false trembling voice, and was told that she once had sung in the church, strong and clear. I feel that I'm not in your mind anymore, and not at all in your body. And I feel I will sometime write to you, now and then, in the next twenty years, just write bits and pieces, as you say, in this language.

You came into my life, so you are there, however you change. My beloved. Gleaming now, like what? Like fire. I see myself as "the native woman" running with tree for the white man's fire, stop running and the fire fading out. My beloved.

Saw a Fassbinder-film yesterday, surprisingly bad, "Effi Briest". When the love is stopped by outer reasons I cannot realy cry, see it as a lack in the love, that the love wasn't there, actually. They were wise, the old ones, to create the enemies of the love as unavoidable destiny: poison, war, prison.

Seeing a lot of Thorkild and his nice wife for the time being, they like Marijke very much. They have a surprisingly milieu, so much bourgeois, so conversasing, teachers and psycho-analists and other dull persons, Thorkild mumbling harsh-nesses between the teeths, sending me sidelong looks. Then we hear music, loud, loud, dreaming, not about each other but about the same, in the middle of all the coffee and the slogans of the day.

I am rather lonely, but not bad, the physical presence of other beings are warming anyway, "the cowshed warm" as Adrian Leverkühn called it. But the most important in the last weeks: I'm reading Céline, *Voyage au bout de la nuit*. It has been in my bookshelf for years, have red the first page several time and put it away again. And then a day, just like it happened to me with *A la recerche* ... (which you admire your whole life but only adore in a certain phase?)—a day I read the lines I've never red before and you see what is showed for you: a knock-out of precision and truthfulness, falling drops of a lyric beauty, surprising as an angel in a low-class-pub. I suppose you know the book. What effect did it have on you? How do you remember it?

Send also little notes from some weeks ago, also about literatur ... So few words we have, after all, about other persons efforts.

The picture of me in your chair in your London flat came out very hazy, a ghost-picture nearly. Now I cannot find it.
Steffen is drinking very much for the time and playing billiard all day, his language reduced into burbs, and his feelings and thoughts too, of course.

And you, my sweet, how are you this day? I guess bad bad bad. Poor everybody as you said. I still believe in next summer, I don't know what it will be like or where or how or together with whom, but I still believe in little caves of oppersite life.

Yours forever
Elin

CHAPTER 11: Letters 35, 36, 37, 38, 39, 40 (1976)

In the Bath

Letter 35
(Handwritten)

7. jan. 76

The beloved

I've just talked to your wife—for the second time. You are in bath now. I don't believe that you phone me. I cannot understand that you make this ending ugly and ridigiously. This was no week-end-affair. I've been mourning, you know that. Now you can breath again: I am angry. Finally you have made one more woman angry and disappointed, your picture of the world fits—your *herbarium* is in order.

Beyond the anger lies the love. I will frame it, our love—in silver as I did with your amulet and wear it around my neck.

Elin

Letter 36

London
13th January 76

Direst Elin,

DOLOR DOLOR DOLOR. Phone is disconnected. Bad time here and difficult to explain. Continuous squabbling with *Esposa*. Children suffering. Funds sunk to nothing and Agent sells nothing. Publisher sulking. Driven to work on novel he asks for, with superhuman effort got back into it, have been squashing the bad things in it, trying to let it breathe, now have first 50 pp and last 30 pp and some stuff in between. American publisher would make offer on 100 pp continuous. Might also on this truncated thing. Trying to get it off. Trying to get out from under it. Tiempo malissimo.

Frightful Xmas Day followed by ghastly New Year, smashing glasses, long periods of no-talking, no smoking or drinking, just working and fighting and sleeping alone, feeling so miserable that I can see no hope, wake to more fighting, more struggle—what Grandmaster Ross calls Marital Rhubarb.

Into all of which or towards the end of which, for beyond that sourness it could not go—ping!—in comes your sad waspish note, smelling of cordite. Mourning. Anger. Don't be angry with me, dearest. Wanted to wrap myself up in your cloth, which hangs over back of my work-chair, wrap up in that, swallow the calmative, take candle-holder in firm grasp, go to sleep and never wake up again. Afraid even to utter your name, so low have I sunk. So forgive me. Did not want to go to you penniless and broken up, only asking for 4 weeks non-stop in bed, so that loving you could cure me. Did not want Marijke there, even. Tried a few times to phone you when phone was connected, but gave up as sons came clattering in, wife banging back.

Time in bath in morning is not even peaceful time, but drawing of deep breath between troubled sleep and beginning of another troubled day of no-talking, overt signals of extreme hostility. Perhaps you are familiar with the pattern. Silence becomes preferable as talking only leads to shouting and quarrels. Nothing goes right here and she sees no good in me, and bills pile up. Bile also.

So. Now comes some light. Ross has Book Club friend who is looking for someone to select volume of short stories and write short introduction, for which £1,000 paid, half immediately. Which means I can pay rent, overdue, electricity and gas, phone bill, various loans, can even buy bottle of wine and packet of Gauloises.

Not walking much, just asittin' here, working, sleeping, in this room, sorties down to the kitchen or into the front room to stare out the window. *Esposa* keeps herself to herself, we only meet to quarrel. I wanted to go to you at Christmas, could have borrowed fare, but she said that if I went out of the flat I could not get back, she would throw my stuff out, destroy letters written to sons. She has become sort of demon. Tried sleeping together with her but it was no good. She says I should be psychoanalysed. Useless, useless, useless. Dolor, dolor, DOLOR.

I wanted to ask you: Why are we right together? And: How can I live in Copenhagen? Don't wish to fall as helpless 49 year-old mess on you. I have no hope here with C. Paul vomiting in school. Night fight here, throwing water on her. Hitting.

Surely with us no week-end affair. You have ruined other women for me. Why not find a tall slim good-looker with long auburn hair, long legs and take her to bed? World full of them, but unfortunately they are not you, the memory of whose manyfold charms rots in me, tending to be perverse, all Lucretian *ferarum quadrupedumque* or wildquadrupedsinrut position: need gone awry (ever read letters Jams Joys wrote to Norah Barnacle back in Trieste circa 1902?). The sickness I have only you can cure. I do not enjoy life without you. Tell me how we can be together somewhere.

I am thinking now of Malaga in April. To meet again in Cataluña, continue to end that *besondern Kuss*. Walk out of the Buñuel Bar again, be glad again. How wretched that life is so short and we can do so little with it. And then to go back to Atepmoc. And stay there. (Handwritten:) For 3 months.

Rosenberg having dropped novel option, now open, another "serious interest" shown. "The centre holds," de Warr declares rather grandly. Am meeting Producer this week here, with view to me writing new screenplay.

I was in a mess and could not move out of it because of bills, no chance of funds coming in. And now all changes. In addition, the extracts of the novel might be placed in US magazines by Agent, or sold to publisher with respectable advance. So it looks as if I am rising out of debt. Towards what?

Towards you. Your responses are always right, always unexpected. Now comes rage and mourning, an unlikely combination. Please tell me what can happen to us. I have not had a happy day since you left here. No *Kuss*, no *Knepp*, nothing of that nature. Sorry for long silence. Blame Sister Dolor. Now I am beginning to know the bitch. Choke her off. Please understand why I did not call: understand that there was almost nothing of me left to call to you. Pain tooth. Swelling eye. Cannot go out. Cannot drink. It drains hope. I refer to recent past.

Now all that changes. Am going now to try and phone you from Rhoda's place. Making arrangements for payment of our phone bill. In this damn city of 8 million souls, it's like being lost in a forest when you're without a phone.

How are we right together? Can we live anywhere else without this split of me here and you there? I am not Strindberg: cannot give up all to write. Could I not work in Atepmoc? And you be there with me. But it would have to be with Marijke. Tell me, in your strong belief and by your strength, how a possible future can be arranged? Or can it be arranged? I mean a future of us together. If that is possible.

(Unsigned)

Letter 37

Finsbury Park
22 Jan. 76

My dearest Elin,
I write to tell you that the financial dark clouds that have been hanging over me for some considerable time are now rolling away. Had lunch with Ross and BCB (ex-Philadelphia); hard on double whiskies in the Colony Club he upped offer to £1,500, to chagrin of the Board. Have now more or less made selection for book of around 350pp., working all day yesterday and part of night. So that all that remains to be done is to have matter typed out or photostated, and write Introduction.

In meantime spent night of chess at Wandsworth near infamous prison, from where I tried to phone you—Thursday night. Had some drinks in the County Arms where we drank with Ross a century ago and you found house called "Bornholm" facing the Common. Next morning, following many whiskies of preceding night, found I had only pennies in pocket, walked across Lambeth Bridge into City, where agent had just received TELEX from New York to say that publisher had made offer on 30pp of novel, and was offering $5,000 advance. Irish movie deal seemingly on and gent of bulging eye even inquiring what sort of fee would be required. Agent and he are talking today.

Bought 2-litro bottle of Italian wine and was working all yesterday, bethought me that I too have an island that I'd like you to see; very small, windy, treeless, surrounded by freezing sea full of mackerel. Gaelic speakers—a language that goes back to time just after Homer. Fifty miles off Galway: Inishere in the Aran group. You would like it. Jackasses bray together at night as if the Little People had frightened them. Couple of hours out by boat. Take you there one day, maybe with Marijke.

By this morning's post comes letter offering me £250 fee to act as adjudicator in Hennessy Award for short stories, run by Irish newspaper quite in the manner of Carlsberg. Our fare to the islands, with free brandy thrown in.

What should we do with this year together, my dear, when your "dubble nervousity" (DR job) will be over? The casa in Atepmoc will be free from April 1st, when your Islands Brygge time ends. By then I shall have finished Book Club stint, Hennessy chore and—hopefully (working well)—the ur-novel on Ireland in the Thirties. May even have $2,500 US advance banked and no money worries for a year or so. Would it be good idea to meet in Hotel Cataluña, spend days in Malaga, kill each other *mit Knepp und Kuss*, with white wine at Buñuel Bar, and then down to Atepmoc and hole up there for 3 or 4 months?

I don't know deadline for film, supposing it comes off. I wouldn't need any reference books. The Bulging Eye speaks of summer 77 for shooting in Ire. Don't know what size fee Agent would demand. No knowing what sort of money available to Irish film industry. Don't know what deadline America would ask for novel. Would have to do film first. If begun in April, might be ready by Xmas. Family go down when school ends towards end of July. We could leave mid-July (after hard work) in either Bornholm or Inishere, and then come back here. With money one can arrange anything. Tell me what you prefer. Or what you want.

104

As a matter of fact I don't believe I can last that long without seeing you. A TRIPLE Nervousity! I take long bus journies to this and that bar, stand at the counter and drink this and that. Wondering why I am here exactly. We could go to Amsterdam, spend weekend there. Since you are quitting your job in early April, I don't suppose any furlong from DR is due to you?

How strange that Cataluña room and the *besondern Kuss*. How beautiful you were in Café Español where we drank gin. I thought: *With her anything is possible.* I mean in life, that progress in love and despair; in that melancholy which belongs to animals (part of us) who live an instinctive life always, in (per Yeats) "the exultation of love." This of course is ... your parsnips? Write soon. I miss you.

(Unsigned)

Letter 38

København. den 26. januar 1976

My dearest Fitz

This letter will be difficult to write and difficult to read. As you see: in bits and pieces. How much shall I answer, how much shall I explain, how much shall I interfere you (and your family), how much have I changed, how much do you ask about, how much do you want to know. Difficult stuff. Send it here in bits and pieces.

"Don't be angry with me."
I am not angry. By writing the waspish note the anger disappeared. I am not angry with you.

"So forgive me."
I have forgiven you. Through a long time, already, I've forgiven you. If it seems different for you, is it maybe because we understand the word forgive in different ways. I understand as to leave that subject which demands the

105

forgiving, to keep silent. Maybe you understand it as: to forget, to go on as nothing had happened.

"If you go out of that flat you can never get back"
Don't you live in a better way by the end of the world, moss-eating, than there, where your children get ill by DOLOR, your wife turns into a demon and yourself are reduced to a mumble???
As when Coppera says so, is it then a threat? Or rather a fear of seeing you return—after a while—for the 7th, the 9th, the 13th times?
Am I too rude?

"Tried to sleep together but it was no good"
How do you begin to make love, how do you begin the caresses, how do you touch with your own tongue the other tongue, these tongues just shriming the most evil they know?
Do you walk out of your own room, creeping up in her bed, demanding your "matrimonial right"?
Or does she go into your room, shaking her breasts??

"She says I should be psychoanalysed"
She is right: it is needed.
You are right: it is useless.
Are there anything dearer to you than your own impossibulity, your own sorrow?

"Why are we right together?"
Your tactics, unchangeable:
You put a false question, which force the opponent to put a false answer. Or to be silent.
We are not right together. When you assert that, by asking about why we are, you close one eye. Even you know, that everything were not right—not in London. And in Atepmoc only by the burning wish that it should be. In Atepmoc it became true. But one is only initiated once. After that must the initiation work.

And I have closed the other eye. My deceit, as I called it in "*Cri de Coeur* of 12.11.75." I reduced and reduced myself, my revolts, my objections, my speed, my rashness, sharpness, my rudeness, my thoughts, my world. First because of my need of language (Atepmoc), after that because of your need of answers (London).

And I doubt you will ever learn the other forms of life together than what you see in the first meeting: A woman, an adored shell, silent, waiting for you, hoping for you, following you. The continuation, what comes after the first meeting, you hate and despise. Or hate and fear. Why?

You know it. I know it. You don't have to say it. But tell me, if you can, if you want to, WHO or WHAT gave you that torturing idea: that you must be the strongest, the wisest, the deepest, that one with the greatest rights, the superior, the possessing one? Your mother? Your odd country? A certain laziness at women you meet too often?—Why did you meet just them too often?

"And how can I live in Copenhagen?"
How can you live in London? How can you live in Atepmoc? How can one live?
At the Buñuel bar you said, that at the bottom—and pointed down into the kitchen—that at the very bottom did one find the reality, and that you desired nothing more than that.

"Paul vomiting"
Once you wrote that I never more should confess about making love with another. Nevertheless such confessions are your innermost lust.
I beg you: Never more confess about your children's sufferings. I get sick.

"Surely with us no week-end affaire"
Surely with us no week-end affaire.

"And go back to Atepmoc. And stay there."
No, I don't dare, I don't want to go back to Atepmoc and stay there, in your house, for a long time, depending of you.

The pattern, that one you know so well from connections with other women, would catch us in the course of a week. The end would start immediately.

I see the addition "for three months" and get lesser guilty.

The common sense. Maybe my answer fits you rather good: Here and there and on and off.—I am so awfull serious. The seriousness *for* you, you love. The seriousness *against* you, you hate. That simple is it. Isn't it?

"*Your responses are always right.*"
Are they? Also now? And are they answers? Aren't they rather the next painfull step?

"*Please, tell me what can happen to us.*"
I do try.
But when I write these cruel things I get disturbed by my own dreams, wish-dreams, start to doubt all over again. Maybe, maybe I misunderstood, maybe I remember wrong.

I send you some few notes from the time in London:

F suppress me, knowing and not-knowing. Never before I meet such a suppression. Yes, maybe from Marijke, but she is my child, I can form her.

We lay in bed, the conjugal bed, that I would have sworn never to do, I escaped into the front room in the morning. It is difficult to ignore the suspect, the ridiculous by laying in another woman's conjugal bed. And the children. What do they feel? What do they think?

I told F about my greekish dream, about my dream of us together. I told it in a clumsy way. He answered: "I am too old for that kind of thing." I asked: Yes, but how then? He answered: As with Hannelore, here and there and on and off.

Dinner at Rhoda's. F's silence, R's confusion, my loneliness. The dinner. I'm going to explode from all that petty forms. I ashe on the plate. F removes it. I could have hit him. My aggressions in the front room after, balancing between the attractive and the scandalous. F sees all of it, also the acting in it.—F's definition of the bad picture, my shock over his depth and precision. Why does he never use his intelligence on himself, on his own situations?

F wants never—quite automatical never—what I want. Him one can only follow. Everything die if one goes against him. We went in Queens Wood. I maybe find beauty to the left but he has decided to go right. Immediately everything is spoiled, killed. No response, no obligingness, not at all any commonship, only self-will. And the worst: No curiosity (WHY I wanted to go left). A strange need of love. A strange lack in the feeling of, or respect of other being's reality.

We walk on the roads. I pick a leaf, bright, deep-green, beautifull in shape. It ends in a kind of thorns. I say: It is like me, beautifull and prickling. F is unpleasant affected and says nothing. This is the worst: the refusing of knowing me. I tempt and tempt him to ask: What do you mean by saying that, but no. He never asks. He talks. Or is silent.

When I am wrong for him he is frightfull: he punishes me, doesn't touch me, doesn't talk. And when he starts talking again he is malicious and nasal, with a memory as an elephant and a penetration as a snake. He, who is a passionate liar himself, he suddenly remembers any statements which can prove, that what I've said or done, not only are stupid and wrong generally, but also incorrect and false according to my own norms. He is frightfull. And I am not afraid of him anymore.

I think he disgusts types like me, is only fond of the very young girl's unconsciousness, deceit for me who is 33.

The hostilities stopped yesterday at World's End. But the spell is broken, the dream of the opposite life is fading out. It doesn't hurt me so much now, but later comes the despair, later, when I need the dream and none is there.

22.12. He is so weak, not even strong in dreams, rather stubborn, I think. I like weak men and I like strong men. But I don't like weak men when they act like strong men, or try to grow bigger by making me smaller.

26.12. I cannot avoid to shatter him: slowly, steadily and necessarily.

12.1.76. I think I am through it. I am so released. I feel like a house, ready for new banquet. The dream is over but the same is the nightmare. I am so released. In a certain place, in a certain room I will love him always. He changed me. There will always be a certain room for him in my heart, my house, my life. They are art fellow, these "real men", they never get used to women, from us they are always hoping of peace and agree. They will hunt their own dreams untill they die from it. But everybody do so, I guess. Fitzy, my love, how I loved you, how I hoped from you, how I waited and waited for grandiose reasons to show up, reasons which could justify your arrogance and egoism. I did not see them. I saw mostly weakness and tyranny. But it doesn't matter. Only think, it doesn't matter. In a certain place in me I will go on loving you.

Enough, enough.

If you mistake my cruelty for spitefullness, if you degrade my sorrow to insult, my quickness to superficiality, my courage to stupidity and my love into nonsense ... I might really kill you.

Then you called me on the 13th. And everything started over again. But yet in another way. I begin to see a pattern now, I begin to see what is possible and what is not possible. Maybe it begins now? If you wasn't exactly you, with your hate to the truth, I would believe it.

Reality:
I'm going for Greece mid-April, alone or together with Danish friends. I will stay there, in a neutral house in an unknown country for 3 or 4 months, working. Marijke will be with me for 3 or 4 weeks. This is a 15 years old dream of freedom and work.

I fervently hope you can come for some of the time. Or for all the time?? Then we can make love together again, on and off, often maybe, at the sea maybe.

I think I can get you a place to live in Denmark, if you want to. At a humble castle, at Elsa G, a well-known cultur-lady and her husband, an american painter. Then we could see each other frequently. I'm not sure you would be particular happy by that. But I think the time has come to live on your own,—hasn't it?

Now I have "reproached of you because I fancy that our intimacy entitles me to do" ...

Can you hear a kind of love behind all this?

I think I can.

(Unsigned)

(On separate sheet):
One thing is missing in this long cruel letter: all the moments I loved you. I wrote so often about that. And it is still true. But there was something else which was also true.

26.1.76

(Handwritten)
Dearest F

Just come home from work, exhausted, hungry. Had promised myself not to go home before ending that difficult letter. Would continue at home, and do so. Marijke is at Steffen's because I should have been at a party tonight. Wonder if I come. Your high letter came. Just red it. It will be difficult—even more—to go on with the cruel letter. It will.

But first, my strange dear F, Congratulations, so fervently, my love. You deserve it. You are a splendid writer, I mean novelist, because I cannot imagine you as a play-write, with plots and all that, excluding your discriptions, your waves. But you will show new sides of your talents surely.

Oh oh oh what can I say to you letter? Once more: Congratulations. What a foolish word. A foolish american song sounds in my ear by that word. The refrain changed by an early american friend of ours into: Congratulations and masturbation ... tralala la ...

The tone in your letter, so elevated, so happy of being able to *take me away*. For some months or so. Maybe even for a year! As you decided to take Coppera away, once, for the Atlantic

Island. But also, my sweetheart believe me, also it touches me so much to hear you say that. That's your way of being good. I see it. Certainly I would prefer not to spoil it. Believe me. But I am not to take away. I am too big, in all meanings. Your calculations of money sounds strange to my ear. Since I was 16 I've earned my own money. The Great Animal is shut, once more. The bag belongs to yourself, or to Coppera and the kids. I don't know anything about what kind of arrangement you two have together, but certainly it does not belong to me. Tell me can the phrase "an instinctive life" be mistaken for a confuse life, a life in bits and pieces, a life of the same theme, over and over again, always losing its taste—after a while? I look at my words and see that it can not be mistaken. It is synonymous. An instinctive life, the life of the animals, is repeating the same over and over again, bits and pieces, always hunting. Confusing for us only because of the memory. The memory call us to order, demands the bits and pieces turned into a progress. Do I choose the right words? I write in the dark, inside the dark, in a strange language, avoiding stiff dead words as responsibility, obligations etc. Trying to make this stiff words alive again by showing you the inside meaning of them, the private meaning. It is words which might be *for* you, not against you, it is your words. It is your life, your alone-life I'm talking about. Or alone (only) your life.

I don't doubt that Coppera is wrong for you. I don't mean anything about if you should leave her or not. Yes, I mean you should leave her, but not because of me, but because she is wrong for you. Because you are wrong for her. Because you are wrong for each other.

If you are.

But imagine you, returning to London, to Coppera & kids for the 17th time, after having fun and disappointments with me, *makes me sick*. DOLOR DOLOR what hard words I write. Do not despair: You would hate me in the course of a week. My mind is sure, but my body, the memories of my body pulls in me. No, it is even worser: it is also the memory of my head, which pulls in me, the imagination of how it could be, if it were a little different.

Fitz, my Fitz, I see much good in you. But I've lost the belief of a possible future for us together. I cannot be depending of anybody. And you know only dependence. But little caves of Opposite Life? Not *taking* anybody to opponent's places? Little caves of free life, working-life, love-life? Is it possible?

I can't end this letter. Wish you were here so I could repeat this hard words to you, seal them with kisses, open them with kisses, make them eatable and understandable.

Yours
(Unsigned)

CHAPTER 12: Letters 41, 42, 43, 44, 45

Dusting the Icon

Letter 41

Finsbury Park
September 6th 76

My dearest,

Missing you, moistful. Don't know how to contact you now. Am writing to Nørre Søgade and Islands Brygge, supposing Steffen will forward nothing with London postmark, supposing Denmarks Radio in ignorance of your whereabouts. Thorkild Bogen's address somewhere in your voluminous correspondence but I hesitate to look into that, as the last epistle nearly killed me, as perhaps was its intent. Have only just recovered from its spleen, but thinking of you most often than not, everything else finished, even novel of sorts which I have been struggling with off and on for years, now into its last smallish third.

Leaving for 10 days in Ireland. Coppera leaves for three weeks in Spain from September 18. If you are out of Greece, could you come here then? Nothing since, but hating you, now missing you, missing-hating you, now just missing you, idea of seeing you again almost Too Good to Be True. Hated the way you cursed me in your letter, for what I tried to show, delight, turns out it was the wrong path through the wood Inebia. But you hated Malaga once when there with Obey & Co and I showed you another Malaga. I thought I could go on doing that, not confined merely to Malaga and the docks and the Buñuel Bar under the sea, but apparently I was wrong. I forgive your letter. I want to see you again.

Have stowed away smallish sum in Atepmoc, want to take some months off to get into next work. You said once, wrote, that if I wanted you, I'd just have to say where and when and you would come. Write c/o Clery, 33 Hatch Street, Dublin 2.

If you can reach me before 17th, say, thereafter here. Do write. Please do write. I've thought about you every day. Tried to phone from Wandsworth when I could have reached you in Copenhagen but left it too late, and discovered then (when I thought to phone again) that you'd already left for Greece.

If you have somebody else, if you are happy, don't bother to contact me. I am unhappy, missing you,

F

Letter 42

No address, undated
(Autumn 76?)

Dear

A strange synchromous: The night before your letter came, I wrote this other unfinished letter which I put by. As you see: I answer letters no matter what the letterwriter wants.

As you see: I am not happy and not unhappy and "together" with somebody else. After all I am happy not to be unhappy.

I smile when I read your sentence: "I forgive your letter." It is like you haven't red it at all.

What more? "Love always." Yes. I send love for you, too.

Elin

(on separate page):

Dear Fitz—found this stuff by clearing and remember that I promised to send it back once.

Your blue suitcase dissolved in Berlin a tuesday evening in rain. From the suitcase dropped the Ouzo, from me tears and mensesblood. Since then I've recovered my strength but the suitcase is reduced to a memory. I've given up to see the white dressing-gown, bought a new one yesterday.

The time at Naxos was very instructive. I learned—among other things—the difference of writing poems: the impulse of one moment. And prose: to keep the thought clear for a long time, and describe more than own states. Repeated also the lesson of loneliness. Did you ever receive my letter from Naxos?

I'm going to move. I'm going to live together with a cultur-sociologist with whom I've nothing in common. He is 43, medium-drunken, Marxist, IK 160, I guess. Me he finds incomprehensible, is still fascinated but exhausted in three months, I guess. When the sociologist throw me out I move into a collective, I guess. I cannot stand anylonger the Private Life's mortal structures ... As one says.

Steffen has disappeared in a cloud of fascism and ironical distance. He loves only his child. It is good. Marijke doesn't like the school-life, she got alarming sure instincts. I've given up my job to november. A year after I decided to do so. Do you remember I wrote about it to you last summer? I make my debut with 2 poems in Gyldendals Poem-Anthology (modest but honourable) and 8 others in a literary periodical. The poems got very fine opinion from the literary reader. They are all approaches.

(Unsigned)

Letter 43

Truss City
September 28/76

You, YOU

didn't recognize stamp, type-face, even my name scrawled in your handwriting within, in package privily delivered to my bedside by eldest son before going out to work one drizzly morning, poisonous contents hardly more consoling.

No, never received your letter from Naxos, an island not marked on the primer atlas here. And if I cannot find that, how then can I find sense in the fact that you smile when you read purse-mouthed embittered little sentence to the effect that I "forgive" your year-old letter, loaded and primed with malice and selfishness, a deliberate tearing apart of any good times we ever had, in favour of an unrealized (unrealizable) notion of fitness and order (your fitness, your order), that not only attempts to make a farce of all our times together, but shows you as a bitch, willing only toads and rodents on us. But, under the hardness of that letter, I am not even entitled to write "us." Lost, then. And then the smile again, condescending, on the feeble "Love always.".

Well, then, why damn you too forever, beaming whore—*Strahlenbuhlen*—how wrong I was to smile, be touched. "An April face, simultaneously laughing and glowering: variably cloudy." Your face. I thought of it on your birthday. Regretting that I had waited so long, let you slip away.

Nothing in common, I read, IQK 160 sociologist, "going to live," I read, "together," I read, "fascinated but exhausted," I read, "incomprehensible," oh sure, whore. Were I given to it I'd howl. Was "faithful" to you all that time, twenty years of marriage dissolving not in mensesblood and Ouzo but in real blows, real blood. Or, failing that, freezing bucket of water flung over bed at night. Hard sayings. Bad before Xmas but even worse after, evening out in the spring, during all which time I remained constant to you in the only way you can remain constant, in the heart, if you can know what that means and can read it without that dangerous "smile," or baring of the teeth. And then the crowning stupidity: a Collective, and a Danish one at that, the most stupid of all. Christ. I dream even of being poor Steffen Krähe, seeing Naxos doesn't exist, and nevertheless you are on it, damned whore, plotting in midst of "lesson about loneliness" (a lesson not learnt very well, apparently), to meet IQK 160 and ... "live together." It is a marvel that your right hand didn't fall off when you wrote it.

Hypothetical fidelities are useless, to be sure. Systematic tearing out of parts of refuge very hazardous occupation unless alternative bolt-holes ensured for subject, now hypothetically stark naked, skinned like a fox, running at top speed towards hypothetical bolt-hole which is withdrawing itself at roughly the same hypothetical speed, hear the rush of air, hear the hypothetical scream. I bow down lowly before you and strike my breast and wish you all the very worst with your IQK 160, with whom you have nothing in common, as runs the curious legend.

Sorry I kept the shroud so long, not knowing where to send it, seeing Naxos doesn't exist, it was grand company. In the bad times I wanted to lie down and chew it to bits, maybe eat it, piece by piece, looking at your intimate hair, hair from your

117

body (that evasive vessel) that you once sent, when you used to write—used to write, just say come, and I (you) will come, as you did, as good as your word, to here, to the window embrasure, to World's End pub, to the Spread Eagle, the only possible places I can drink with you after the Buñuel bar in Malaga, discussing life under the sea with you, where I always live with you, calling ASTA ASTA oh oh ASTA again!

Sending this to Islands Brygge so you can spill your coffee or better still choke on it, fearing to send it to Nørre Søgade, now sunk under Sortedams Sø, where IQK 160, hearing it fall into the letterbox, will instantly smell a dreadful smell and burn it straight away, not allowing it into your hands.

And having said all that I have said nothing. Except that I thought of you very often, daily even, seeing you as dearer than them all. Another great foolishness of your letter, that presuming epistle that did me so much harm, is the calm assumption that I have scores and who knows hundreds of Trulls in a woman-infested past. Not quite accurate. Give very little and very rarely. And now disliking faces, voices, the outside, the air, the ground, faces, voices, the flat, the voices, food, noises, voices, the day, the night, dreams, the mornings, noises, myself most of all, foul recepticle of all those ill things, illness undiagnosable but mortal: the illness of a life without you.

Well well WELL. Enough of that. Finishing novel for Skinflint-Shylock and have one beyond it, mostly written by you, to date, already accepted by American publisher—a novel about Berlin (where blue suitcases tend to dissolve, Ouzo bottles smash) and Copenhagen, that I began to put together as soon as I saw you, the abominable night I first saw thee.

Thought—being in this matter apparently incurable—to live with you again, live somewhere with you and finish it with your help. Perhaps I should put all such foolishness out of my head, live with my family.

> Meet you in Amsterdam when this chore is ended.
> Meet you in hell.
> Love all the same.

F.

Write sometimes. Say you forgive me.

Letter 44
(Handwritten)

Copenhagen autumn 76

Dear,
Just received your letter. Don't understand half of it but very well the tone, the message. I like your anger voice in a way, it stops your self-complaints for a while—admire in a way your on-going madness (learning what!). I met IK 160 in Copenhagen after Naxos, friend of some friends. I fire him tomorrow, prefer to repeat again my lesson of loneliness. Yes, I'm selfish. I want to survive but I'm not very clever to it. Yes, I'm selfish, want to create my own world, don't want to go into another person's world, don't want things to be showed to me, want to see things myself and then—if possible—share my views (?) with my beloved. Not possible. The dream: to see the same, to share the views in common: total impossible. Well, enough of that, as you say.

Send you my poems even if you don't understand the words. Most of them is about "you," things I learned while I learned you to know, one, the longest, is for you.

A very bad winter is in front of me, no work, no money, an unhappy child, no love, great fear (this sentence might be from one of your letters). Yes, I'm mean. I smile my purse-smile to myself.—Please send *Irish Times* article, and after that your books. Brought your Bildung, Nabokov and Céline and Chinese poems with me to Naxos. They nearly killed me, this books, it is, in fact, good literature.—I hate my lovely apartment, I hate to live alongside my child, we kill each other, I cannot, seemingly, live together with anybody. The bad thing is, that being in collectives are a bit more idiotical than other thing. I hate other beings. A question of preference to be hanged or drowned.

—Then, in between, I make myself beautifull, and go out in town, seeing the dreams of men in their faces, half tender, half cunning, they imagining to start a new life without changing themselves.—

Yes, that it is a pity that you let me wait so long, let me slip away. But you did. Didn't come to Xmas-time, my heart broke, I was all waiting, the last last hope. And you didn't come, I slept in the new bedlinen alone and you were not there. Well. You must have good reason for not coming.—

Had a frightful time in Naxos, half mad. When I twice a week talked with the other foreigners I could not find out if I was dreaming or awake, I watch their faces to see shadows from my words, skreaming you name beyond the locked doors, drinkly madly. I came through it at Naxos, it is over now, I only tell this things in order to pain you: My love to you is an embryo with all the dreams in it but without a name.

—IK 160 a rather ordinary man behaving most strange. He wants to keep me but escape himself, he says he loves me but fucks other girls all the time—they have no faces he says—he wants to be together with me but drinks himself into a baby-point when he is (he is not living here), he wants me to make the gulfs in himself smaller and they grow and grow. A very typical being of his time, never met such one before (closely). Of course I cannot change him a bit, my Florence Nightengate-days (and nights) are counted.

Very late now, 3 o'clock, cannot sleep, thinking of tomorrow, writing to you, which now finally, finally is the same as my own "mean" thoughts.

Elin

Letter 45

Copenhagen, 5. january 1977

Dear Fitz

Got letter from Atepmoc yesterday. Believed for a moment it was from you. It was from Pernille. Seemingly they have a nice time, built house bigger, having house warming party with Spanish neighbours.

And you, how are you in this days? I hope—I don't know what I hope. I hope to see you once before we die. I'm in a strange state. Not good. I'm living of social-support, very little money, plenty of times, some work, much dreaming. It is years ago since I lived so near to my nature, it is not even "nice," it is what it is: NO comments. Yes, one. I suffer from moral scruples, knowing other people have same dreadfull

120

lifes as me when I had to earn money. My fellowmen (quasi-artists living on support too) say: "No, we are guerillas, showing the world is mad" ... etc, etc. But I still have this pietistic suspicion what is nice to myself can't serve other purposes, too. A question of course and effect.

I cry very selden now, because of you, and when, I do it is with a clear point in my mind, knowing: "Now Elin cries for Fitz." As to blow dust from an icon.

You changed me. How could I ever forget you. I like to be poor. I like the slowly moves of poverty. Plenty of time, everything is meaningless and important. You had it, that slowly beauty, especially in Atepmoc.

So, my dear, so I think of you. Don't give me an harsh answer: "Ha, so you think of me now, when all your lovers have gone." They have not,—or they have. It is not the point. They were 1 or 117, it is not the point. The point is that I can't stop wondering what happened to me on my 33rd-years birthday. Tell me what happened. Once more.

Elin

PS: It should be longer this letter. It sounds fatalistic. and superstitious. I'm not, I'm glad I think. Marijke get used to the school (well, so and so), Steffen all right, easy, my friend. I look better than two years ago. Maybe I will be an acceptable writer, maybe I will encounter ... Again.

(Handwritten): Write me a letter.

(Unsigned)

CHAPTER 13: Letters 46, 47, 48, 49, 50, 51, 52 (1977)

Copenhagen Dobblegänger

Letter 46 (1977)

Finsbury Park
7th January. 77

Dear Elin,

Coiled up in the regularly recurring bad night. Another sun on morning wall for the first time in ages. Sounds of milk delivery preceding it in the dark and then the slither of post arriving, a gas bill and your Express Letter this morning. What can I say, what can I repeat? Back into the past, back into the past. This culled from last year's Atepmoc Diary:

"No post since Xmastide. A sunny day today, bilious with trench mouth. Stench of unwashed humanity very offensive to nostrils fastidious as mine, the PO presided over, most incompetently by no other than our good amigo Lauriano the unclean Piscean, up to his tricks, i.e., doing nothing in the PO (not even sorting himself out), while a crowd of Waggada Waggadas are loudly demanding mail from Barcelona, Albacete, all over. "*Hoy nada!*" he says with a fearful grimace. Reputed to be An Informer. So the good old Denunciado system still operates, though the Generallissimo is old and enfeebled. A while back a Madrid bomber was sentenced to two lifetimes and 80 years, just to be on the safe side; two others garotted for killing Guardia Civil. He (the U. Piscean) positively will not wash and oozes alcohol from every pore: Casa de Correos smelling of baffling mix of birdcage, tannery and brewery. A consumate master of the labial toothpick trick, shifted from one corner of the mouth to the other sans hand, while he is "thinking," thinking up more lies. He refuses to deliver mail, you must collect it yourself, as does Nils Bud, his hair standing on end. An unwashed odour permeates the Casa de Correos there beside Aurelio's bar where you astonished two campo-workers with your Red Indian headband and gin-drinking ways, one night. Lauriano's hands tremble, his gooseberrycoloured eyes dart here and there, he drinks Sol y Sombra (cognac & gin mixed), toxic as meths, shaves with a cutthroat, bleeding profusely into mounds of dead letters. A melancholy scene. Melancholy: the projection of a psychic state (Gustave Moreau): the Hump."

Thus then. And now? Been screwing up heart to write to you for ages, thinking of you often, for all the good that does you. Hal Ross, with whom I sometimes drink in Harry's bar in Hampstead, advises immediate departure Copenhagenward. Siege on the impregnable without. Fitful dreams of freedom, none hereabouts and that's for sure, hesitate to depart Atepmocward, recalling nightsweats on floor-bed, continuing nightmares, face pressed to the glass for hours, choking with no alternatives, distaste for all and sundry, backed up by a kind of dread, *Furcht, sich sekend, führend Traum*, in a word: *Niedergeschlagen*.

Novel en route to printers, proofs by mid-February, publication delayed in order to enter for new £7,000 prize for unpublished matter. Popeye relapsed into thoughtful silence after shelling out £500 movie option, money which he says he can ill afford, shooting, he says, to begin in spring. I do not believe a word he says—a Dream Merchant.

Have applied for writer-in-residence post at University of East Anglia, was interviewed by no less than six Professors *and* an inferior English novelist. Skinflint publisher, with two black Labradors in the office, more kennel than publishing-house, urging me to try and write new (!!!) novel in *five months*. He has disembursed funds for me to retire into Atepmoc but most of this is already consumed by rent & rates, sundry bills.

Doubt whether I could face Atepmoc alone. Doubt if I can face anything without you. Sourness since your departure. Tried in a feeble way some alternatives. Both spoke the wrong language. Need your mixture of neo-German-urEnglish with some Danish thrown in for good measure, to keep me awake. In a word: dreary and joyless time, with parts of teeth falling out and eyes worsening, hair uncut in years. See how two years without you has harmed me. Missing the vibration, shaking you in the folds of the curtain. Please tell me what we can do. Heart pumped dry.

Last year an awful one, only relief was finishing novel, best work I have done yet I think. Your name in it and also Marijke's. As part of the general impossibility, I see her, little pet, as an impediment, cannot ask you to join me anywhere while she is there with you, not to Atepmoc nor to East Anglia in spring, if it comes. A dreary spring lies ahead, a no less dreary summer, and a winter to follow whose complexion it would be folly to predict, cold anyway. Days of perfect misery in every respect. Dead waters.

And I without one word of Danish (except "*Skaak!*") to offer her who might hate me anyway. So much for moral scruples, so much for hindrances. Cold feet, cold hands, feeling half-ill all the time, feeling as if *gone away*. But where? I don't know. Apart. Nowhere good.

A time, times, and half a time. 3:30 now and the sun setting somewhere behind the Queen's Pub, that flatulent old bitch Victoria who sucked red jujubes white. Been down with flu, abed hoping never to rise again, not been out for a fortnight. So it goes.

BBC repeating Coleridge project in the spring. Overseas Service arranging interview next week. Weak with despair doing it, then suddenly it all changed, pick up any page and it sniggers back at me. Would be glad to see your poems with a Danish dictionary, please send. Perhaps more hopeful bits of me are stumbling around in there. Nothing much of that here. I look at the destitute cowering in the chilly cement shelter.

Walked one whole night near dirty river Thames down Chiswick way, crossing and recrossing huge unlighted bridge, nobody about, no cars passing, glow of distant City like Hellfire beyond bare trees, overcoat abandoned in somebody's flat, an animal screeching in death-throes in a park. Remember the foggy night in Atepmoc when we heard such screeching in the hills, happiest second Sunday of my entire life, the days we didn't rise until evening—"that slowly beauty" in old Atepmoc, put there to remind us that our life is -short, just clinging to the rock. Nothing much has happened since.

You ask what happened at your 33rd birthday. You took a

124

blow and have never recovered from it. I took a blow and have never recovered from it. I didn't want to recover from it. You are continually walking into the room, numero 33, of the hotel overlooking the Malaga Cathedral, that Renaissance-Baroque pile of brown freestone with its 18 chapels opening off the aisles, one of Pedro de Mena's polychromatic wooden black-painted saints looking much out-of-place, a Negro saint in wood; you are lying naked on the white bed, I am with you, we are at peace. All else is just *Ausswallung*.

Wanted to show you the best walks in the woods here, forgive me, Elin dear. I asked on the phone whether I could go to you on Xmas 75 but you said no. I forgive you. The rest, I curse it. Blame my ongoing madness, as you call it. It has been going on, but silently. The *besondern Kuss* has never ended. I miss your voice. I kiss your neck, give you gooseflesh. You are dancing behind a pillar in the Dutch queer's bar in Nerja with a glass of Bloody Mary in your hand. I wanted to ask him about *Homo Ludens* (Hal Ross stood once behind Huizenga at the British Museum reading-room) but it seemed compromising, the Dutch being tinged with a slightly ceremonial reserve. I am howling (silently) in the Buñuel Bar near the dock. We have a bottle of uncorked white wine. I forget the name of the hotel. Malaga swallows us up. I swallow you up. You swallow me up. Sister, ghost, happiness.

Is that what you want me to say? After your cruel letter, its intention perhaps misunderstood by me, fearful of attack or doubt from that quarter, no quarter, then not, but as now again, shivering, longing. Write, tell me that I should do to live again. You, you, Elin.

F.

Letter 47

jan. ultimo. 1977

Dearest,
Have started so many times now on an answer to you. They all turned wrong out. I don't know what to answer, that's why.

I am glad to hear that novel is through, that you are lesser poor now. Please send me a copy when it comes out. I can pay for it if the free-copies are few.

I am afraid that not more hopeful bits of you are wandering around my poems. Send you two anyway. They are called "Rørvig or Aphrodite Goes Home" and something like: "To be matter of the burning limiting shape." Look at them, if you like, we can translate them once we are together.

I am writing rather continuously, finally. It cannot be the novel I hoped, poems again. I don't know when I have to take a job again.

I send this non-answer typed on paper because nothing is worse than silence (to me anyway).—I don't curse it. I try, feeble as you say, to bless it. It. The hotel was called Cataluña.

Yes, after Naxos I tried to recover. I am afraid to disturb that new thin calmness. Let us once more hope in the coming summer. Keep me informed of your planning, keep on the possibilities of seeing each other again, once.

Elin

Letter 48

Finsbury Park
Mid-March 77

Thank you for your birthday greeting. I was 50 in March. Your 35th coming up. You will be 35 in April, moistful, variously showery.

This two years since we first met, your birthday our first together, helping Florencio the "Italian" (as a true Spaniard he didn't care too much for the joke) to erect the tall chimney, cornering the Pastor's champagne, the day we couldn't eat in Jesú's place in Nerja, when you danced with Bloody Mary behind the column, when you were jealous with no cause, and I felt sick in the car, you were quarrelsome and boots were thrown before sleep, around 5:30 or 6:00 am. Next day we didn't rise until 8:00 pm Sunday to walk in a mist. Nothing much has happened since. We were same ages as Isadora Duncan and Gordon Craig, having themselves a high old time in Berlin and elsewhere. He had no money, she came to sticky end.

Here the Transport slogans are formulated with eye-catching appeal across the fronts of double-decker buses. A W7 heading for Muswell Hill Broadway has VICE BOOM like a boast. I see a W3 with I HATE MY BIG BOSOM (Ex-Beauty Queen) setting off. A country strikebound, having lost its Empire and now about to fall behind Spain in per capita income, is about to loose its head. I creep by the National Westminster Bank (the Bank of England is putting on a squeeze, no overdraft for Mr F). Walk over the thrice accursed Royal Common Ground called Alexandra Park where you lay down in the sun, in a previous existence. Past the ghastly View Bar with scaffolding up in front of it for nineteen years. Spring growth trying to burst free, birds seem to believe it's possible anyway. Cats glide through the weeds. Geese in the slime of Clapham Common.

I move around. All the futile abyss outspread (*éployé*): some clever Frog held that the elements of chance and the externality of the real is expressed in that word: *Eployé*. Could be he was right.

East Anglia turned down application, so no East Anglia for me, I am glad to say. Sorry to hear you were unable to come here. Went into one of those European-style self-service-and-chess places in Hampstead and saw dark-haired tall girl in T-shirt like you favour, something of you in her, gave me a shock. With Ross in another bar last Saturday, I went to phone, was accosted by girl sitting alone, not sober, smiling at me and "Hello", if you please, a come-on. *Your face*, the posture, eyes, more or less the look from the eyes direct. I said, "Do I know you?" This she took as rebuff. Either drunk or drugged or just lonely, looking to be picked up, and part of her (superficies) was you. Had notion that your ghost had addressed me through her, told Ross, "Elin is sitting back there, or her double." Ross wanted to know why I hadn't accepted offer.

Innishboffin, small (200 population) island off Donegal, is having "Informal Cultural Festival" for week from April 22, and I have offered my services to *Irish Times* to write two articles and possibly some sketches, if they would pay reasonable fee. A Mrs O'Dea runs a guest-house. Have also approached *Guardian*. Could Mamma/Pappa Marstrander look after little pet for a week and can you raise the sea-fare to Dublin? In course of this week I should have answers from both papers and would then write to Mrs O'Dea asking for double bed. I don't know that part of the world. Irish islands are fine if windy, surrounded by spray and clouds, it's in the Atlantic's mackerel-crowded seas. I'd have sufficient for both of us, you'd just need the fare to Dublin. I don't want to go to Spain, and Copenhagen seems too expensive. I want to see you again, have been sunken in doldrums, a half-life.

No, didn't finish that novel, hardly begun it. Finished the other one, non-rememberings of things past. Late April and all May a very good time in Ireland. It would be like our day in Malaga. The day you looked so beautiful in head-band and drinking gin at Bar España or whatever is left of it. The day of the Buñuel Bar and the rest, a day that was one long *Kuss*. Nothing of that sort I need hardly say has happened since. Curious touchless time. Not alive, no. Family go Spain-wards in late July. As for me, I don't know. Ross often inquired of you. I suppose he wonders how I can keep away from you, often wonder myself.

Your Fitz

Letter 49

København, den 21. marts 1977

Dear Fitz,

Thank you for your letter. You too are wandering around in a fancy resteraunt in the midst of Copenhagen. Called "Summershoe". Sic! J'Espoir told me. Asked if *your* ghost was english-speaking but he didn't know. I'm mostly in, writing rather little, rather empty, no music in it, having allergi in skin worse than before, need summer badly, glaring out of windows, looking with eyes of memory.

I have to move from my flat-at-lake before the year is gone. New law, created by the Royal Danish Socialistic Party. Sic again. Move or buy it. The flat will cost much, so no shadows of choise. In one way I like that I have to move, just so anxious of being caged somewhere with no light, no clouds, no trees.

The Ireland-plans: During the winter I've put away 100£ for a journey to Rome where Thorkild and wife Helene are living in April/May. I might change this and go for Dublin instead. But I will have absolutely no money left for food and hotels (and cigarettes and wine). The journey to Rome is a 2 weeks-chartertrip with hotel and ½ food included: 110£. And the fare to Dublin is surprisingly expensive: 100£ for train/boat and 130£ for flying. As you see there is a very big difference in price between charter-trips and individual journeys. If you think I should go for Dublin, I will go on tuesday the 19 of april because it has to be on a tuesday. I would be in Dublin at 6 p.m. We might dine together. At Buswell's maybe.

If possible answer rather quickly: can you afford such an arrangement? So I can inform T&H (and myself) about Rome or Dublin.

Elin

PS: You seem very distant to me—just now. (You know the feeling of regretting when reality turns up. One gets scared. And tired in a strange way, in advance). I don't know who I'm going to meet in Dublin, and I don't know who *you* are going to meet, I mean, it's all a bit museumlike, lived through so many times, turned into pictures, symbols, sort of icons one might say.

(Unsigned)

Letter 50

Finsbury Park
London
29 March 77

Dear Elin,
Losing everything, bills pile up, hope declines. Law of Dimishing Returns operating. Your letter lost or mislaid in sorry confusion of papers. Stuck in beginning of work that rises like Rubble Mountain (Mont Klomott) before me—American publisher's deadline this fall, quite impossible

129

for me.

No word from *Irish Times* as to comission for Innishboffin expedition. Remember from your letter the cost of Irish trip, half the Roman trip but more expensive, if I was rolling in money I would say come anyway, but in view of all uncertainty you should stay in Rome, perhaps come here later this summer, or I go to Copenhagen when family go to Atepmoc, a place I have no desire to return to.

This is disappointing. Perhaps you would not even recognize me now, maybe I am somebody else, getting used to being frustrated. Shoes in tatters let in the rain, pullover shrinks, getting teeth fixed, too timid to have hair cut, hoping for better times, digging into rubble mountain. Shortness of breath, sleep alone, doze before gas fire. As rent is raised, electricity bill soars. The grim without, the grimmer within, moribund you might say, hardly an attractive sight, only hope for freedom in the work. The miracle, the funds, solvency, free of debt, that dream.

F.

Visit-Kort: Letter 51

Copenhagen

1. april, 77

Don't cut your Hair
Repair your teeth with chewing-gum
Open up your Painful Eye
and make a secret Move.

My dearest Fitz, I send you my love.

E.

Finsbury Park
14th June 77

Imprisoned here—self-imprisonment (the longest term)—a month, at least, wading in papers, sinking, drowning, always sober, hardly smoking, nothing happening with "novel", just pictures before the cleggy eyes, come and go, what's left but haze? *Nicht ich*.

Yesterday got smashed with Ross in nookshatten Hampstead, Harry's Bar, where you lost the flowers we'd gathered on the Heath. View and Storemont Road, that trail from Highgate cemetery and the Prince of Wales. Met old acquaintance (French wife of journalist, Irish) and asked her how she was. "I am flow-ting in an Osh-un of Nothing-ness." Telling me she is 50 (as I..., married 25 years), adopted son (aged 13) being "pursued" by Suzette, a chess-contestant. None of which can be of the remotest interest to you.

Are you my dearest? I write to try and keep the habit, lit up (hangover) and on edge (Paul at home, writing exams). Woke up this morning after thunderstorm of last night which I heard nothing of, found your note in the cage, in the gloom. Am glad you have called. I was wondering when you would return from Rome. Long continence and immersion in a work that repells, will not move, has made a *Geist* of me.

Have applied to place in Cornwall for Fellowship in School of Fine Arts there, "up to" £5,000 pa, orifice in school, live in town for a year at least. Hope I get it. Interview in late July. Would ask you to come and live with me there, if this comes up. I think of other vague possibilities—Innishboffin that never came to anything, I never went, newspaper did not press me to write articles, so I stayed put. (And always alongside you there, your daughter. Always).

Strained atmosphere of home and obvious lack of love between parents bad for our sons (17,15,13), eldest working as Ussher, trouble with local louts (*Lümmel*), a month ago a gang of 15 set upon him for refusing them entry, tore his jacket to bits (mine given to him after his had been stolen in first week of job), he was uninjured more by luck than design, must keep an eye open for gang, prowling and out to "get" him. Taking driving lessons, has paid over £100, money spent like water, his father's son, nature of my Father, a great spender, when he had it. He should be saving for Spain but isn't, longing for Spain. Permit me a little forced laugh.

Finished the BBC project and await Greekish producer's comments. Page proofs of novel came to publisher's office today.

Family fly to Atepmoc towards August end for three weeks. Novel due in maybe September. Next novel deadline then, nothing much done on it, having expended much "thought" in finding reversed names for places (Madstop, Nilbud, Agalam) now given back their true names. The snow-owls in Berlin Zoo, the house lit up like a ship, Coppera singing "Frère Jacques" (in German) to her sons in the bath, the dark path of Joachim Klepper Weg, the illuminated Little Squirrel bar seen through the trees, the this and the that, all hazy, that is to say, unwritten. Sometimes I tremble. Go about in terror. Nature seems far away. Did you ever feel like that?

Publisher (going mad) talks freely of US reading tour. Unknown in my own country. I say, I'd give readings there. Have never read any of my own labours except to prisoners in Strangeways Prison in Manchester—and indeed would prefer not. It would be nice to live again. Before it's too late.

(Unsigned)

PS: Send me a colour photo of you taken recently.
In the midst of this non-life I sometimes wonder about you, and your small ghost.

CHAPTER 14: Letters 53, 54, 55, 56, 57, 58

The Melancholy Since Rome
Life Among the Rocks (Connemara)

Letter 53

21-6-77, Copenhagen

My Dear

I was very glad for your letter. Have been suffering from melancholy since Rome, interrupted by unpleasant practical demands. The calmness from winter is disappeared. Haven't written for three months now. Have started as freelance "editor" for a publisher with a small inferior "hobby-books"—fits me better than freelance radiojob, which (for me) demands the same effort, namely, as to write myself.

Have been struggling with *The Golden Notebook* (Lessing)—I think I give it up. These foolish hobby-books allow me to stay at home. But the time, the precious time, runs. With this and school-meetings and tax-meetings and social-support-meetings and people who think that I can have a little talk with them, now I am home "anyway" ... I am very angry sometimes. And I know it is all my own fault. You let you disturb when you are disturbable.

My sister is going to be devorced, needing care. I, exhausted in advance, knowing that the devorce will be put off. She will regret. Once more. Not because of love (indeed not) not because of hope, not because of resignation but because of fear for the silence. Do many people doubt about their own existence if they do not stumble over each other all the time?—I think so.

Yes, I too, feel very far from nature. In this days it is one year since I saw mountains, waves, water. Sky and clouds I still have in front of my windows but as a picture behind glass.—It would be lovely if you got the job in Cornwall (on

133

the countryside? no, you said town. But maybe small town, easy to walk behind you?). I could visit you there. We could walk, and talk a little, and maybe make love, who knows.

I can't find out from your different projects and their deadlines and due. Send me something when it is published.

"Alongside her, always her daughter. Always" did the man say—alongside him mountains of impossibilities crowded among 3 sons and a wife. I don't remember if I told you that Steffen and I alternate every month to have Marijke. Since Naxos this arrangement has been going on. Very successful, M happy for it. And Steffen. Keeps him alive. Gives me some freedom. We are the very picture of the happy devorced family. I'm serious.

Well, dear Fitzy, I must start working, this time on a small book of the new Data Processing Language. If Cornwall fails we might take a cheap charter flight for Malaga, just one week, together. It is very cheap from Copenhagen in autumn-time. Be glad, dearest. I don't know if I am your dearest. It doesn't matter so much any more in a way.

Do you remember very well, or do you not remember at all your own letters? In the very first letter you wrote: I write to you, dearest *Schwesterlein, in order to get the habit*. So you see what I mean by saying: it doesn't matter so much any more. We are in each others lifes, however we use or not-use or mis-use this factum.

Elin

Letter 54

18. aug. 77

Dear F,
Wonder why no answer on my letter?
Has a radical change come?
Wonder if I might see you in October or already in September. I have some money, I can keep off for a month. Thinking of seeing Atepmoc again, re-coming.

Will write to Pernille if still no answer from you. Or do

something else. Or nothing. Strange summer, blowing, grey, no lift in weather. Wonder if new Ice Glacial is turning up. Thinking of you, still dayly, reduced from always to sometimes, without direct pain but still sometimes with this weakness in bones as that sunday afternoon before the windows in Finsbury Park.

Hope for answer of a kind.

Elin

Letter 55

Finsbury Park
13 October 77
Thursday

Dear Elin,

Have been travelling in Ireland since mid-July and only came back here in early hours of Tuesday to collect typewriter and stuff, sorting through mail came upon your note of August 18.

Will be returning to Dublin for promotional party tomorrow and then going North East to try and find a place to work in through the winter. I too often think of you but cannot get beyond that. No longer any urge to return to Atepmoc. Finding London (as ever) intolerable. Discovering my own country rather late in life, my own people who speak in a language I cannot understand (the Gaelic). Have been looking here and there.

Will send copy of novel of sorts.

Would settle for less than love. I think of little pet speaking only Danish, me speaking no word except ... have forgotten it. How would the three of us survive in one flat? My 3 perhaps miss me, away now for three months and about to leave again. I say come for Xmas. They say, It's a long time away.

The London air releases some black substance. Wiped it off windscreen of friend's car outside Rhoda's place in Swiss Cottage, the flat where we once went to bed surrounded by flowers.

This letter is no answer; I cannot give an answer. Weakening perhaps, putting you out of my vida, weakening, weak. Very tired this last year. It seemed a very long cold year.

135

Only now getting together some force. Please write to me in Dublin.

F.

Insight Cards: Letter 56

folio two. No. 8 An Hooker
Photo: Beehive Hut circa 6th cent. A.D. Bealadangan
Slea Head. Co. Kerry. Connemara

Dearest Elin,
Living here among the rocks. Sorry for delay in sending enclosed, will try and write, you always on my mind but I can't write letters. You write me, tell me about what you make of the book.

F.

Letter 57
(Handwritten)

No address, undated.
(December 1977?)

Dear Fitzy
I wish you a happy new year.
I'm expecting, now impatient, to receive a copy of the Irish Novel. Will you arrange that? I'm still living here in Nørre Søgade for a while.

So strange and right you settled down in Ireland—wonder if you still are there—if this letter reach you. Will not write more this time—write soon—send that book of yours.

Elin

PS: What means: "Would settle for less than love?"

A Card of Mourning: Letter 58
(Handwritten)

No address
May 78

Forgive my silence.
My sister is dead. I'm living in Rørvig mostly in this weeks,

136

Kos-journey suspended. My mother is near going mad, I don't know myself how to be normal again, I'm freezing in his lovely summer.

She commited suiside, flinged herself out from a tower. I'm sick, we are all sick, please write something to me. She was so lovely, so weak and lovely. Pisces.

Elin

CHAPTER 15: Letters 59, 60, 61, 62, 63, 64, 65 (1978-79)

Connemara Abandoned
Plans for the Kφbenhavn Crossing

Letter 59

Finsbury Park
London
2nd June 78

Dearest Elin,

Your sad note of a while back to hand. Was that the sister who tore her shirt off your back and you and she fought like wolves before Steffen? Have before me a letter from June last year telling of her plans for divorce, her disturbances, and now a year later and she does that. A terrible business. For you and your poor mother not to mention your father, both gentle types as I recall you mentioning. I know about six who did it over the years. Martin, younger than I, knew five—one girl trying for a year. It's not to be understood, really not. I felt freezing for you when the note came, was reading suicide Tadeusz Borowski the man from Auschwitz who did away with himself in Warsaw in 1951. His wife was in Birkenau. He was living with another woman. Then your letter dropped through the letterbox.

Larry Rivers incarcerated in Reginae Coeli in Rome, sentence coming up. He could get 5 years. He walks a minimum of 3 miles every day in the prison compound, spirits unflagging. Ross and I are attempting to help with sworn statements for sinister Advocato here. An even more sinister criminal lawyer is assisting from Rome.

Was thinking of you in Kos. Sue Fay was in oily Athens last summer with her young son, said Greek men were pigs, somewhat better on the islands, epileptic Australian drowning, hippies fornicating on bus before the young boy, keeping in touch with the Classical Past.

Should we not try to live together? We are drinking gin at World's End, taking beer in the Buñuel bar in Malaga under the sea. Were they happy times? At all events nothing like

138

them has occured since. Stay bright.

Truth to tell I want to see you again. Have never in a way been unfaithful to Grassy Place, the long walk home and you like a fire lit in me. On what harbour or railway station or airport could we meet? Where could we live? Tired of language I cannot speak or understand, but tired most of all by the English as spoken hereabouts, and Ireland I can do without. Whereas you not, or so I fondly dream. The two Sundays we had in Atepmoc constituted a sort of Eskimo marriage, the almost interesting mist a honeymoon, and you telling me about your apartment. Nørre Søgade, disappointed (you claimed) with what you were saying, whereas I was delighted with every word, because it showed me a life I wanted, showed me a spirit that I liked (not too hopeful), though "like" is too weak a word; a life, then. It sometimes seems to me that these types of admissions are lies, saying them is telling lies, but perhaps you know better what I mean. There was an edge of something that I have missed ever since. Be hopeful. You wrote once that if I wrote "Come," you would come. I cannot ask, but I want you to come. Perhaps you can. But where? When? Answer.

F.

Letter 60

Finsbury Park
London
23 August 78

Dearest Elin,
3.00 am on 24th more correctly, leaving for Luton Airport at 4:45 am & all going well should be in Malaga by midday today.

BBC TeeVee film to be shown on September 20 but Agent assures me that he can arrange private showing before that. Could only get one-way ticket at such short notice, family returning here on 7th September. Would like to be able to fly from Malaga to Copenhagen then but will probably have to return here so will be in Copenhagen later than hoped.

Long state of drifting persists. Persisting in false choices, no alternatives offered as far as I can see (not far). You say I'll find you changed. Me also I suppose, more baffled than before. Did little work on Irish inner-travel book in Dublin over past two months when I had hoped to finish it, finishing something else instead. More wrong choices. Could we work together or is that now impossible? Are you still alone? I am.

Not going to bed tonight but up playing poker with Nico and now feeling inspired to write what I'd prefer to say face to face, supposing I have a face, or you. Will end cautiously here and will write again from Atepmoc, supposing it exists.

Love still, long absence, confused longings all circling about you. As before,

F.

Letter 61

Finsbury Park
London
2nd January 1979

Dearest,

Forgive long silence, going again through a peculiar time, swimming under the surface and never reaching air. *Verstörung:* means something between distraction and bewilderment. "There are moments when I am able to look without any effort through the whole creation (*Schopfung*) itself, which is nothing but an immense *Erschöpfung*." Thomas Bernhardt. At bar 97 the second theme returns and is elaborated.

Against all odds (drunken Piscean Postman never delivering mail, since sacked, following Denunciado, the biter bit) your letter reached me in Atepmoc, thrown in through the door. I never saw the postman, the post office was always closed. I didn't like Spain this time and may not return here, certainly not to Atepmoc. Then I had your Danish book and letter of November, around the time I saw you or your double walking away from me with a dog in Queen's Wood. I don't know what expression "you" had because you never turned your face, your shoulders (if it was you) looked resigned. I sat on a bench and watched you go. It was odd to see you walking there. What were you up to?

I wanted to be in Copenhagen for your publication day,

then wanted to write a long letter, then thought that a telegram might be better than nothing, then the time went past and I sank deeper, or remained in about the same stage of submergence. That was October 1st.

Will be in Vancouver for a reading next month and would like to return via Copenhagen to see you, before we disappear. All the money I had last year is gone and I am back to nothing again, which is very depressing as you likely know yourself. Only gleam of light is that Ogrebuch was accepted by publisher in pink shirt and this comes out in the spring. The underwater swimming effect is result of all this. Also the silence. Holding my breath. Not that I forget you or anything like that.

I hope that your book not one single word of which I understand except the name *Michaux*, does well and that you are happy with it. I have a copy of my first book for you in its new format unposted since November & I send it now with my poor love.

F.

Letter 62
(Handwritten)

Copenhagen, 5th of March 1979

Dear Fitz—
Would call you but get dreadfull nervous by imagine Coppera or kids answering, or you, in a bad mood, so this note instead.—Congratulations with saturday 3.—I write, so you should know, I'm not in Andalusia (if Larry is in London now and told you so). I think it's a bad feeling, thinking of people another place than where they are. Everything went wrong, so I retired to Copenhagen yesterday together with Marijke. Had hoped to rent Pastor's house, but impossible. Trying now to find a job for a month and then, about 11th of April, go for Greece. I believe Lesbos (Sappho).

I'm so nervous. My next book just accepted, I got 10,000 Kroner from the State's artist Fund, fear that all money disappears in wine and bills before any travel is possible—already nearly the half of it has disappeared.

I bless you my dear, bless your Canada-journey. Strange to see Atepmoc, your house—couldn't again find the right one—has it a brand-new door, or—on the contrary—a very old one? Went to Canillas with Anna, Marijke, Pastor & Wife, drank 103 in that dirty bar where I nearly fainted before. It was raining. Finish.

Love from Elin

Letter 63

Finsbury Park
7th March 1979

Dear Nervous Elin,
Yours of this morning to hand, and glad to have it, good news to hear that you are programmed for second book. Is that 10,000 Kroner?

Was afraid you thought my last letter a devious adieu, with all that stuff about another language, another people, which it was not ever intended to be.

Elusive Larry Rivers arrived back by coach on Saturday looking bronzed and fit, as if he had come from vacation in Bermuda and not jail in Rome. He came up with Ross and Melanie and daughter Kate for dinner and I missed a word from you, as he had just opportunity to say he had spoken to you, and liked you, and that you were sending a kiss but he wasn't giving it.

Am currently struggling to get money from Skinflint, owed to me from television rights. Also attempting to rough-out outline of possible piece for stage, based on radio stuff I did long ago on assassination of Trotsky.

Vancouver reading is still on, May 2-7, and I hope to come back via Copenhagen, but not if you are in Lesbos. Today with your letter came telegram from Washington University asking if I would speak there for $1,000 before or after Vancouver, who are only paying $100. Coppera is going down to Atepmoc around May 20, so I would have 9th May until then free to go and see you, provided that you are not too remote.

Have passed proofs of Ogrebuch and now await reading copies, with drawings to be passed. Hoped to have travel book ready by May but it does not look so good, agent did not like it and it is now with BBC Belfast, 50 opening pages. They pay near £500 for hour stereo with repeat. Astronomic electricity bill to be met and await similiar gas bill, as snowdrops come out and garbage strike ends, though garbage still spread everywhere, a mountain of it in Golden Square, waiting only good weather and arrival of rats and plague.

Now turned or gone (as they say of eggs gone bad or "off") 52, hopes not eggsactly declining but fell backwards onto gas fire one night and thought I had damaged something crucial, but X-Ray said no. Indoors for weeks on end, breathing difficult, mobility impaired and only now returned, but stabs of pain on Mayo knee still persisting, walking in West End it gives out, and I hobble (suddenly old) to Finsbury Park bus-stop, carried home cursing weakly. And this only the beginning of the third or final stage of La Vida, most of it wasted, or slipped away, slept away.

Am sending telegram to this fellow in Washington University today to say that *before* Vancouver is okay and hope to be free from around 9th or 10th May to return and take ship across and see you, who I suppose still exist, more or less. Will you be returned from Greece by then or can you delay departure if not yet departed?

I believe sea was frozen around Copenhagen and you could walk to Bornholm. Atepmoc rather ruined for me for some reason too, perhaps absence of you, walking twice by the bridge near the winnowing-place where you put your head on my lap and we listened to the chorus in the little valley full of songbirds. Door is oldest door, which I exchanged for "new" door, shifted to house below, the man who is Gastarbeiter in Swisserland. The level where you once walked, being "lost": i.e., away from me.

Have raised my reviewing fee and now get reasonable whack but postal strike in Ireland delays cheque due to me. All this says nothing much. The sun shines for a change. Martin has almost finished German effusion for publisher, due I think this autumn for Frankfurt Book Fair. Perhaps they will ask me over. In which case I could break journey. Bad translation of Bildung, and English paperback edition due in fall. BBC transmission due in interim. For the rest, it's all bills, bills. Sitting here chewing interior bile, where all hope reposes. I wonder what your flat is like and how much room is there and what you do with yourself.

Our Hotel Residencia Cataluña in the Plaza del Obispo is closed up, but I suppose our ghosts, quite happy, still abide there, looking into the depths of the extraordinary full-length mirrors on the doors of the hanging-cupboards (the bevelled edge indicated their oldness) in which we came and went as in transparent water, on the fourth floor centre room (Numero 33), facing the Cathedral, where people were just going into Mass. It was Rogation Sunday, 4 May, 1975. We had great gambas at El Torotto run by the chap Hannel knew, since closed; and draught beer at the Buñuel bar in the harbour, which is really La Sirena, run by a queer who was most reluctant to sell us a bottle of white wine for the hotel. Café Español was closed then, is now only a third of what it used to be. You drank gin, looking marvellous on that day, the few of the last happy days, the many we had together, do you remember, my dearest? Write and tell me where we are, for I do not know exactly, or even generally, having vanished to myself.

F

Letter 64

16th March 1979

Dearest

Thank you for your letter. You ask me to tell you where we are. I think apart. This said without bitterness, pride or even relief. I noticed, when I opened your letter, that I red the article first. This must mean that the interest has become greater than the love.

I think our affair "conducted in fake German" was a love-affair. To me it was. Immense. Not before and still not since such a shaking. But it *is* behind me, it would be a lie to act like it still is present. Strange enough it has something to do with my sister's death. I can't quite explain why. Maybe all shocks leave you changed (as my meeting with you did). Well, honestly, I think it happened earlier, rather did the death of my sister give me a new name for my sorrow which untill then was occupied by you. Yes, the grief got a new name and *claws* when my sister died.

Yes, it was a affair of love, then a affair of sorrow, then a affair of literature and now hardly that. Forgive me, dear, I'm certainly not scolding you. Certainly not. I will try to tell you that just like a chair f. ex., or a picture, a dress—not fitting the room or the figure any longer—still can be loved (you find a particular place, a particular ocasion) just like that you become a welcome in May.

Of course you are. I think I'm at home but make a call to be sure. And not sure of anything else. *Come if you like to see me.* Strange that you can avoid to understand that it is a long time ago I *and you* gave up ever to live together. Much longer than your last letter which I can't find—strange because I keep all letters.

The scholarship was 10,000 Kroner, 1,000 I use in 2 weeks. My poems is very much regarded from the criticism and other authors, not orient.

I write them because my prose is so false in tone. In poetry I can avoid it but it is rather exhausting, yes, and you get a bit mad, yes. I'm not sure they are good. Yes, sometimes they are. In whole they are good as a whole. I turn them over in my mind with tip of tongue in cheek.

I live alone or together with Marijke. Very selden lovers. Was in love in 1977 with a young painter, a beautifull liar. He was too experience-greedy for me, I too thought-greedy to him, it ended with an interrupted call. But he heated water when I was freezing and put dried roseleaves in it. We also overate strawberry together. Now he is waiting child with a broad-hipped silent girl, he says he loves me (and don't doubt). Wonder if I'm turning into a ghost-aunt, a shadow-aunt.

Yes, I remember Café Español. Looked for it when I was in Malaga with Marijke, couldn't find it. Hotel Cataluña was still there, drained with rattling shutters. I remember the elevator-man, sniffing as a little dog in all opening, when he

145

followed me in the elevator to get the poncho, you waiting on the steps of the Cathedral, watching me. I crossed the arms around the poncho with the same move as when you cut bread or pray. Sometimes I think I remember everything.

Your steady absence forced me to write 3 years before I else had started. This 3 years did you not take while they was there. They are there of course not any longer. But only think what after-waves.—I think we should stop this unreal correspondence when you have answered this letter. Yes, I would like an answer now when you no longer calculate. Yes write me that letter. "If you can't be magnanimous, be mean," as you promised. I stop now, stop looking in dictionary (so slowly, so clumsy). If you want to see me then come in May. Or another time. You will be received with tenderness, curiosity, respect and who knows, after staying a while, with love.

Elin

(Handwritten PS.): This dense, strict tone is un-intentional. Can't put 4 years of life into 1½ pages, not able to make it longer in this language which is un-real and heavy to me. I *think* I loved you more than you ever understood—and think I already regret the very last 2 words. I don't think it is true. But it was. I've tried to be so honest and tender as possible for me, all the time. Has it succeeded? And I think all this farewell letters has continued for years!

Telegram from Spokane, Upper Washington State: Letter 65

HOVEDTELEGRAFKONTORET 1150 KOBENHAVN K–8.5.79
SZCXC UDC079 RMR 7481 QRF0494 4-075714E127
TDMT CHENEY WA 20 07 0804P EST VIA RCA

ELIN MARSTRANDER
NORRE SOGADE 254
2100 COPENHAGEN

ARRIVING PANAM 6PM WEDNESDAY MAY 9 COPENHAGEN
FROM WASHINGTON CAN YOU MEET
  ITZ

COL 54 2100 6PM 9

146

IV

Kastrup Airport, Copenhagen,
London, Malaga, Atepmoc

CHAPTER 16

The Strikes of Regretting

31st May 1979

You weren't at Kastrup Airport. No wonder you weren't there. I'd arrived four years, six days and then 24 hours too late. You were alone, brooding at Elsinore. I booked into Østeport Hotel, signed in for a Japanese receptionist, walked up and down Nørre Søgade, your corner top floor window as I took it to be, by Wiedeweltsgade, Jens Juels Gade and Abildgaardsgade, the main drag of Sølvgade and the Jewish secondhand shop Rideudstyr selling lace-up boots, ladies' oldstyle hats, leatherwear, by Islands Brygge bus-stop. It became dark, cold. I waited for you and Marijke to appear on high antiquated bicycles, but only three swans winged in over Guldanden and the traffic flowed over the bridge.

I walked down a cobbled street that runs parallel to yours, Jens Juels Gade, my knee getting stiffer and stiffer, I couldn't have a drink in case you came, thought to add something to the note but feared I would run into the mad woman below, who had been watching me through the window. I went into the wrong flat, saw you had left, a poor flat, tidied up as though you had left for Greece, I opened a notebook and now it wasn't your handwriting. Then in the hotel, now definitely become an awful place, I phoned your number and your voice answered "Fitz" at once. And then you are on my lap and saying "Bed".

I woke this morning remembering that there was a small note with your letter and found it with old Bank letters in the waste-paper basket and am returning it to you.

Could we not try to live together in Atepmoc? The place is transformed. Could we not work there? Another winter in London would finish me. Atepmoc is a dead place only when I am alone there, Not with you I mean.

Now we are travelling in the little red train from Hillerød to Helsingør, past the cut hayfields of Kokkedal, a region of misty woods at Vedbaek, cyclists not waving mounted on high old bikes are drifting alongside the train. We are taking Hof beer and herrings at Humlebaek Inn, looking towards the Swedish coast, a white nuclear station. Single dogs are prowling near the woods, wheat stubble burns in the emptied fields, creating long black strokes. Now we are off to Rørvig via Hillerød and Hundested. You are swimming naked beyond the second sand bar. Dragonflies flew behind the dunes where I took you again. The ferry came on time, you dozed on the upper deck.

The lunch in Humlebaek. The little harbour with the nets drying on the low walls, clean fishing boats docked, one setting out to sea with a bearded chap waving from the poop, the thump of the donkey-engine meliorating over the water. The Danes were secret sailors (witness the stir and excitement on the ferry to Bornholm). I pretended to jump into Humlebaek Havn. Were we not walking into eternity along the fine Humlebaek sand? So strong then the sense of my great lost luck returning, us together again after four years apart. Did not my happiness lie there? Did you not feel that too?

You said you wouldn't look back and you didn't.

Jitterbug girls, Danish teenyboppers, danced all night and I drank Martell with an ever-gloomy Scot (only strong potions can cure that gloom), observing elderly couples waltz and tango through the night, while a half-cast vocalist sang falsetto like a girl. I rose at 6:00 am in the cabin full of Danish jitterbugs, the only one stirring, apart from beer cans rolling in the scuppers. *SS Winston Churchill*'s steelworks groaned mightily but presently the white cliffs of Dover hove into view, with jet fighters in attendance, and soon the torsos of Doverportworkers pink from unaccustomed sun, and so home in taxi through the extraordinary light, and wine ever since, not sober a day. Drank with old Ross in that Hampstead bar where we brought flowers and lost them, to late chess, loglike sleep.

Odd in a way that you had no affairs, or *not many*, or "very few", as you so delicately phrased it (sailor's amusement at sea?). You said that if we were together you would have affairs *at once*. "Come at wance," you cried in Chrisostmo's Bar, "or I'll lick all the phricks in the bar!"—every inch the young whore on the edge of a strange town. It's you loving part of your own city and disregarding the rest.

You stroll out of the bathroom and sit on my lap and then deep *Kuss* again at last, joining up with Room 33 and the mirrors of Hotel Cataluña and you said "Bed". The candle burned all night. You had stood at the street door of 254 and watched me get out of the taxi. When I went up, little pet was asleep, the candle burning. What might it have been like if the three of us had lived in Connemara? But that's only dreaming.

31st May 1979

Coppera returned yesterday from Atepmoc bringing among other useful things (103) your lost letter of April 16, 1976, from Naxos, beginning: "It is Good Friday in Europe today." You write of huge, flat and hot stones, small sandy places, plateaux with grass: in a word, potential love-arbors.

You tell of Greekish men hunting women like dogs. Out of every folder now Elin's letters (cries) fall. Martin writes of returning to Köln where his young love lives, trying to meet by accident (to see if the gods still know their work) his once-and-for-all Ulrike, "the being who so seriously made me fall in love with love itself, a pattern I haven't escaped since then" (we are now in Köln in February 1979).

"Later in Berlin, she called, pale as ever. Taller even"—why did I wake up this morning recalling these lines? Smiling all night in my sleep, at your letter? Dancing alone in the front room to Bob Marley's "Jamming" played over and over? Ben at his breakfast (orange juice) says I am Jekyll & Hyde. Speaking to you on the phone creates much the same … disorder, induces smiling habits. You poured into very tight white slacks with some sort of hook at the thigh, made up for the street, the watchful old babies in hooded prams. In drunken Thorkild's flat, being blasted by Haffner Symphony. little pet in a pet because we spoke too much English in the street, running from the Shakespeare-quoting chap. You in the Nerja Dutch queer's bar, hot with unfounded jealousy, your own, dancing alone behind a pillar with a Bloody Mary in one hand. Smile-inducing imagery.

Strange then the face raked by tenderness and voluptas,

151

sustained (torn up) by *Kussen*, mine I should add, that last time in your flat. The lure, your amulet, a charm against the night goblins. I hear below (we are now back in Finsbury Park in May 1979) the crash of empty milk-bottles breaking in the dairy where workers in blue coats are goosing each other, forever nicking yoghurt, orange juice.

Last night, not sober, I told C of my Copenhagen visit. The only reason for flying twice over the Pole and Grøneland's icy wastes was to see you again. The long walk by the promenade and Rasmussen in stone could only wear you out, make a night of love impossible. We caught a No. 1 bus to Central Station. I didn't tell her any of that. She said "I'm glad for you."

CHAPTER 17

Notations in the Void (1979-1980)

Copenhagen
8th August 1979

Dear Fitzy,

It is impossible for me to come to London. I couldn't never write a line in that apartment. What I would like very much is to follow you through Era. I doubt that "passing as your secretary" would pass, but it is an old dream in me to travel with you in Ireland, sleep in Buswell Hotel and so on. Write to me if the journey comes up and I will try to raise some money.

The Atepmoc suggestion is tempting in many respects. If you go there late September I'll try and visit you for some weeks, I've only seen the sun through the windowglass this summer, am pale and skinny in work.

You never divide hope from reality, and you are not a happy person. I always divide hope from reality (try to) and am not a happy being. You refuse to see reality and I am hoping wrong hopes. This goes on: Wrong moves, failured gestures. Will it ever change?

It's Marijke's birthday today, 10 years. I woke up, in a very nice way: Sl-o-u-wly placed on my bed from high up—like an insect on the hot streams of wind is placed on a meadow. I woke up 7 o'clock. Exactly the same time 10 years ago she (Marijke) came out, little and blue with no scream, me regretting her to live, she regretting nothing; she is all greedy and alive, as I could be if not for this strikes of regretting.

Love, Elin.

Copenhagen
17th October 1979

I talked to Marijke the other day about a new journey to Atepmoc this winter. She said "Oh," and left the kitchen. I found her to my great surprise at the WC, weeping. "Don't mind my weeping," she said, "I do not want to spoil your journey for you." And again I felt, in a guilty way, that she is much too adult.—Next morning came the letter from the State's grant: Nothing.

I was uproared, shall talk with one of the Art Council members this weekend, but I'm not uproared any more. I saw this morning in half-sleep, that I must take this winter alone here, in Copenhagen. It's rather cold, I'm sitting in bed writing this, the room is cold, dimmy after the night. The only hope is to work with stiff, dimmy fingers. You call this dramatization and it is, but it is also real.

Depression. I never saw my white morningcoat again, that one I forgot in London. I think the only way to see each other this winter is the painfull way: a fortnight in Atepmoc, love each other under the threat of a soon departure, look at the stuff together, make some decisions, kiss each other and leave.

This is painful to us and troublesome for the work, but not so painful to Marijke (a fortnight she can take) and the only solution which is possible economical. I'm looking at Peter Tallon's words: that "a meeting settles more than a dozen letters." He's right there. We can seemingly see everybody except each other. Write to me even if you cannot.

Have ate "Higado" and fennel, 2 glasses of white wine. Didn't eat yesterday, was so hungry this morning, it irritated me, I preferred to go on writing to you, but was forced to make shopping. Made it in one jump together with the flowershopvisit, cooked it, ate it, all in one move, I felt.—I'm not looking so much forward for the meal tonight. In Denmark normally they are eating every 3 hours. Hardly is my mother washing up from the lunch before my father is already boiling water for the tea-time.

Love, Elin

27 November 1979

Summery weather here but I do not venture out much. Coppera found a new path that takes you onto our path to Santa Anna via San Anton, and back by the Canillas road, avoiding the village. When you come we will keep to ourselves, live around the fire, or on the terrace; we will be together and maybe not so calm, but little by little, calm.

Quite imperceptibly the place has become kind to me, possible for me; now I can move about and begin to like it, be calm with it. They are most kind people, very unusual people I think. This may have something with working consistently.

Found another bar by the Hulk's place where you bought liver, patronized by mountainy men, drink very cheap, all there blasted by booze, shop annexe doing business at 2:00 am. Another bar nearby. Chrisostomo's, where they discuss the nature of snakes (no damned television).

I go there at night or to Antonio's, the Mulemens' Bar by the cemetery, from where today a great plume of smoke was rising. His rolypoly wife sighs and weeps, thinking always of her dead daughter, driven over the edge in a Landrover by the brother who survived.

Had sardines yesterday. The Atepmoc honey is good, no longer take sugar in my coffee, Larry River's idea, anathema against the processed article—a modern invention, he used to declare. Anything after Napoleon is modern for that grim anchorite, reading Ruskin and Plutarch. He and Miss Mouse are somewhere in Denmark, said to be working at butter—Louis and Marie Antoinette at Versailles, a case of history repeating itself, first time as tragedy, now as farce.

Fiery sunsets set the sky alight now that the rainclouds have gone. Took down flyscreen from bedroom window and put your lucky cloth on the ledge there, your 1840 candle-holder. Found a half-stocking behind the suitcase, the stuff you leave behind, your spoor—also Phrygian cap in the goatshed, mouldy, was going to throw it out but washed it instead and hung it up washed and fresh with half-stockings inside, against your return. When you come I'll collect you by taxi and we can take the journey back-to-front.

27th November 1979

You called yesterday evening, I was burning of dislike of having Steffen listening. English is my love language, and I felt he might hear that, even if I only kept the neutral phrases: Sorry for that cold call. I feel I am never alone, cannot write, not even to you dearest, who wrote me such a warming letter. Oh yes, I can hear through the letter that you are feeling better, much better than I am used to hear. I feel proud and grateful that I—seemingly—can do this to you. Your effect to me is very strong too, indeed, but until now more like a demolition of terms than a creating of new ones.—It will come. I'm younger than you and a very late developed person, I think—so it will come later—after a larger piece of time together with you. If at all I start thinking of you, I miss you so much. So I try not to think of you.

Here is no light at all in the town for the time present, I never quite awake at all. So happy to hear that *you* are awake.—I have very few money. I think I can only come for a week in January. Will try to come January *primo*. Send you a letter about the date when I know it. Is Ross coming in January, too? If—then I must find out the date very soon. That only week in January I want to stay in bed all nights & days—is it possible? I bring some black pretty lingerie, so you can have pleasure of my bedstaying, too.

Once you did a very greekish thing to me. We were in bed and you kissed me, and for a moment—while my mouth was still open—you spit down in my throat, a very *little* but forceful spit, and old sign of possession. I need you.

I am so afraid of the summer—that the plans will come to nothing. I too want a hot place, hate freezing in Denmark or Ireland, but a hot place early summer means Andalusia (where Coppera is in the house in May?) or Greece which you don't like. Thorkild and Helene have some Greece plans, me included, haven't said yes or no. Yes, have said yes, but must talk with you first. We talk it over in January, in bed. Look at money, look at maps! Untill then, sweet paranthetical, hypothetical beloved, I kiss you. Go on working.

7th December 1979

Have ordered a "cargo" of mountain wood from Holy Antonio the campo Saint, seen this morning feeding his mule with breadcrusts and orange peels, a strange meal for a mule.

A fortnight of summerlike weather broke a few days back, giving way to haze and mist in the evenings, with colder nights, but now the good weather returns again. Am avoiding Antiqueran electricians, a trio of merrymakers by night, one of whom sings highhigh like Marchena, the dead voice of Bar el

Molino in Nerja smelling of Sanilav to conceal worse.

Today bought 3 fine big mackerel from Valencia the Fish King, who flatly refused to sell me less, thrust them into my bag, a change from eternal Atepmoc eggs with their yolks like sunsets. Fish King and I roared at each other agreeably, hypocrisy being infectious. Have not walked in some time. Terrace covered in dead leaves. Reading Dorothy Richardson who lived (1873-1957) in Finsbury Park at the turn of the century, cycling from Putney, and passing away in the middle of the century we are preparing to leave.

Make no arrangements with Thorkild and Helene for Greece this summer. We must go away together or stay here together, or at any rate be together.

Maybe I could stay with you in Nørre Søgade in May? Something must be arranged for those times; this is our first and last chance. It would be absurd if between us we cannot arrange something for spring and summer. You are certainly more alluring than the "gleaming" Suzanne B (shoals of those abound), dirty boots and black sheets or not.

I believe the 4 and more years apart were years needed for you to begin work; maybe without me (missing) you would not have begun Aphrodite, no Venus Cytherea. You had to attack from the quarter you attacked, or so I like to believe that I could at least give you that. Spent 4 or 5 overcast days here sitting here digging into stinking old notebooks, digging back into the book I began so many years ago. Little spurts of life, soon out.

Went with Nico (is that tall fellow my son?) into El Maison, Candido's bar. The man-all-music was playing casettes of fandangos from the mountains of Malaga, with his eyes crossed he danced a bit, clicking his fingers, hoarse as a crow, nippy on his feet. He broadcasts on Malaga Radio. Some Danes came in with Nils Bud, among them that terrible, loud, fanged, brutish Dane with whom you would not speak. All hands across the bar, all loud departing, the Whistling Dane last of all, looking shamefaced. We were left with hunters in funny hats, all pissed as newts, or drunk as maggots, wavering on their feet: hunting small birds is an excuse to get plastered.

28th December 1979

Today is Los Santos Inocentes (Massacre of the Innocents), a sort of Spanish April Fool's Day. You are apparently sunken in apathy and general misery, out of which I propose to drag you with both hands. Your note came yesterday and lay on the floor below with a thin aggrieved air. But you are coming.

Will collect you 6:00 pm Saturday 5th, going by bus from here and will take a Malaga taxi back. Bring if you can some ground black pepper and good (Italian?) soap, also if you would, photo of your Grandmother Lemm. Find if you can the names of SS officers who hung themselves in Copenhagen parks around Liberation Day, when Baroness Blixen cycled into town and Danish Kultur began to be respectable once more, if this is not too much to ask.

Last night came a high psychotic wind out of the North roaring behind the mountains like a sea, and blew the deposito-cover and its rock onto the terrace, and almost blew Atepmoc into the sea. Snow clouds driven over the mountains, Ab Oxú looking very precarious and cut-off; today sunny but colder, summery weather here for a month now, in deep winter, hope returns with you.

Xmas tree in the Plaza, I hear, but rarely venture down into those nether regions, where the three electricians lie in wait, run me into a drunken night from which it takes me a day to recover. If I go down for provisions, one of them is sure to be on a tall ladder, waving and shouting. They are from Antiquera and do not know the meaning of restraint.

Cargo of wood is laid on and I have fires every night for company. Your white bowls, Phrygian cap, black half-stockings, and my love almost as tangled as these, all await your pleasure. And I can begin to think of walking on this earth again, you coming here into this endless time which now at last and quite suddenly begins to end.

Tuesday, January 1980

Well, my dear, I'm now in the Aeropuerto, the right one, after an extremely nice and slowly drive. Going down the mountain was like the journey of the hand from the breasts to the bottom: moistfull—as you say I say—descending, lingering, turning and very long. Finally you reach the lowest point and the moistfull stuff changes definitely to anus-stuff, the long journey ends.

Forced the taxi-driver into silence, he tried to start a conversation, me slowly saying: Si-i-i ... to everything and we turned into silencio. Having a huge gin now, I feel drunken, but behave myself decently. Waiters glaring at the writing lady, but I'm not writing—I'm talking—to you my dear—at the Plaza, I'm still at the Plaza, in the sun.

Here is actually dark, vaguely neon-lighted but dark. I kiss your left red arch-ball. I am drinking at the sunny terasse we were once, at the first leave (*Abschied*) in '75. How you were ever allowed to get up here is a wonder, because it's for departing persons only (and you stayed and stay—we were drinking gin at a 100 pesetas each). Now I'm here, having a gin for *135* pesetas if you please, and the very act of having it was as complicated as to emigrate to an unknown country: a iron-gathered entrance where you are questioned how many persons you are (sic!), then is given a huge blanquet, brings it with you to the "bar" (a steel-gleaming office, really), go back with your glass in a luggage-trembling hand, pay the inquestioner with a 3rd newinvented hand and finally escape to neon-lighted dark. People (Danes) are quiet for a change, low-speaking, exhausted I guess, after weeks drinking in hellish Torremolinos. Cheap but low music is going on, melodies from the 30'ties, soft stuff from before the War and my birth, plus a vague smell of Gasolin from the flight which will take me back to the icy moats. I have a rather nice view towards Malaga (in pleasant distance) and the misty mountains beyond.

Copenhagen, next morning, after dwelling in bed = fear of getting up = do I send you this—Express—as last touch. Hope you are in the same state as I left you—I am already nearly not, already remembering, Atepmoc fading out. Kiss you, kiss you. What on earth does it matter if we can fuck as long as we can kiss. Love you.

February 1980

Your Express letter arrived Friday, flung into middle of downstairs room as if still in a hurry. Glad to have it, fearing that you had trouble at "wrong" airport. Forgetting always your calmness, the calmness which I no longer possess. Like the idea of the hand (mine) going down the body (yours). Where, tell me, will we find the calm naturalness that is needed? Never in a way had it with you: not here (twice) nor in London (once), not in Copenhagen in May, either.

Us together in some social scene—Mahon?—unobserved and calm at last—is that possible? Or does it always have to be you weeping at night? To escape into the walled garden with you, calm at last, is it impossible? In something like deep wretchedness here again, strangely enough, I am not calmed without you. As I am calm always with you when I come into you. So that you at the most typical must be the halfdream at the top of the stairs (I saw the back of you just disappearing onto the terrace and going into the bedroom found you smiling at me in bed), you seen nearest to the uncalm—this I cannot understand.

You naked on the boulder at the Second River looking down the valley, or walking naked on the path, or in the water tank, or again smoking a cigarette in the high grass. Or naked before the fire in the back room, leaning forward to blow the embers, revealing your youngness—I know fire, you said. Or with water streaming off your hair and face in the pool that you call Arcadia beyond the smouldering dumps that you call Gehenna.

Some of this known before in other forms—other's forms—now coming again for the last time, or the first time, I don't know; all the others (the few) preparations for you. Calculate that we have known each other for about 47 days and nights, 42 months wasted in between, and a miracle almost that I persisted in phoning Nørre Søgade from Heathrow and then got your new number from the Exchange, so that I had it when I phoned you from Østerport Hotel. Didn't even have to connect through the Japanese receptionist (another in Sands Motor Hotel in Vancouver, maybe a couple of sinister ones from the dream), hot to you straight from my room, and could book out at once, although I had just come in.

Locked the front door here as a rule; but it was unlocked when I dozed in the afternoon (I was up since 5:00 am making the place ready for you, having encountered you as a middle-aged Frau on the path to Canillas, and some kind of a humorist sitting under an olive tree near the Rich Spaniard's mansion, surrounded by children, who waved and called across to me), so you could push it open and, more dead than alive, come upstairs and find me laid out on the floorbed half-dead, afraid I had missed you again. I said: "I don't believe it," and I didn't. You were far from calm then. What does this mean, where is that portent?

Or: the night you threw a glass of wine at me. The day you nearly fainted in the Dirty Bar in Canillas. The afternoon in the Naked Bar with Pepe and his mustachioed wife and the nude calendargirl staring at the Saint, near the cemetery when I was closest to calmness, closest to you, the time we were close to the calmness that is needed.

Of you then, what remains now?

An upended toothbrush, some Macs toothpaste, a goldenbrown hair caught in the table-crack, your prehistoric scent in the bedcoverings. Or: half-into the taxi about to depart from the Plaza, pulled away from me into what I feared was a mess and confusion you couldn't handle; but which you resolved calmly (where was the dog killed, on the way to the coast?).

I knew your face too well; I was disturbed when I first saw it at the bar Perico at 2:00 in the morning and you turned on me that look—the notorious *visu*—that I could no more resist than I can resist breathing. As going from the little square Graabrødre Torv below Bogen's flat, when little pet was peeved because we were speaking English, and walked ahead. And I felt such happiness to be with you both in Copenhagen, your city, which otherwise I did not perceive as being all that cheerful, with old-faced babes in hooded prams and that sad place, the Tivoli Gardens, transformed too; Marijke very solemn riding the small Ferris Wheel alone in the cars one wet afternoon.

February 1980

I read your letter very seriously, almost literally. Often I had not to read your letters too concrete because I felt the hot words as half for yourself, half to me—or better: aimless.

You mention my impatience. That's true, I'm nearly only fire and air (the only water in me is Venus deep in the Pisces sign).

161

Our love affair is not like to see down into a snake-yard, as I said when you were here, it's all understandably and waiting for order. And the order will come. I'm more and more sure of that.

Wonder why you never mention my tenderness. Am I never tender in love? I perceive my feelings for you as very tender. When I write this letter in hand, in your strange tongue—isn't it tenderness then? I feel in many ways that we are back where we started five years ago = Longing. But I know another thing too, today: Never I go into that desperation again which tormented me for years, ending up at Naxos, me half mad.

Today I know that I can live without you and that I want to live with you. Our situations are more alike today than five years ago. I have understood that I never definitely can leave Marijke & S, not really and for ever and ever. I think I will divide my life, have done it already in a way.

I think we this summer should live together for a longer period in order to discover, if that *calmness* needed both for love and not lesser for work, is possible for us to teach.

Then after a long calming summer I go home to Denmark, live with Marijke—then go to Atepmoc with you later in the winter, live with you—then we go back again to our cities, our children—and so on and so on: A regular, calm, divided life untill you, very old, die in my arms—and I go home, very old, and let Steffen die in my arms. That's how we do it!

O, you are so much of a family-man sweet Fitz, much more so than me, you who must live without your family so often. And you go on leaving, go on kissing your children farewell-kisses, go on "disappearing"—how dare you?

You say you cannot understand why I am more real as a half-dream, less (and therefore un-calming) as seen. But it is always like that, also to me, to everybody who is conducted by imaginations.

Have had some bad mornings, worst the second week after departure. I wake up, exhausted. I stay with icecold feets in front of the electric stove, swaying, disgusting my own body, freezing. I sway, touch my breasts with cold hands, touch them hard, hating, hating everything. I feel grief on my own behalf. The cold and the selfpity turn me into bed again, the hate I can tame like an animal on a leash, the hate demands to be comforted. I look at my legs, that are still brown, here in the weak Copenhagen-morninglight they are (compared to the non-colours of the place) still brown. I put the pillow over my head in order to disappear from myself, in order to feel your hands on me, on my body again. Am deadly exhausted, all the sleep has been one long battle against the need of you, your touch and your spirit, a need I must suppress during the day. I will come back very soon even if it is so painfull (after). And then, when it is summer, we go to the Atlantic Sea, and stay somewhere in Ireland near the sea, stay on the very same spot for several months. To reach the calmness if it is possible. *To see if it possible*.

The money for this realistic adventure I get from the Danish State (if I start writing *now*). An already begun book will convince them. You are the one of us who can write, but I am the one who lives in a country where almost nobody can write. My great luck.—Yes, your presence tempted me to write, as I did, and your absence forced me to do—that's no lie.

I do not believe so much in "some social scene". We will never fit together, not in age (that's not true, strange enough we fit in age), but not in nationality, language, upbringing, style, tempo. Solely in erotic imaginations, and—thanks god—in a certain kind of humour which I believe is spirit.

So I believe more in the walled garden. Why do you call that *wretched*? We have the key ourselves, we don't have to stay in that garden longer than we wish.

Your upset letter made me calm.

February 1980

It is snowing today, heavily, huge lumpses are rolling down from the roof, sounding like gigant-animals breathing, clearing voices, coughing. The scenes itself are precise dreamlike: sharp, fixed tumults, even the replics are dreamreplics.

Mr Fimbul with a single arm is gliding through all this white silence. Your feet get tired in the snow, like in sand but in another way—snow creaks, awakes, stirs you. Sand is the summerlove, snow the wintermemory. So I like to be here. All the persons I love, I see so clearly this morning, Marijke for example: lovely like a vase, slender like a vase, rising, sinking, all of it in her eyes.

So *stingy* you are! Not to send me the notes *in case* I do not come back! Everything I ever send you was *in case* I never saw you again!

No, we will never entirely understand each other (and this is not only a question of language), and therefore we will never bore each other, and this is grand, yes.

Strange feeling has grown during the last days: that you have regret your relation to me. I am so afeard. Hear the tape with your voice (very low, Marijke is alseep), first comes the sound of the Atepmoc-cell, then you clear your voice, saying: "Candle burnt all night". Did it? I try to repeat it, but no, it cannot be repeated. It is like a smell, lasting only so long as it surprises.

Wrote two poems last night, while I was so sure of having lost you, the first about my seat on the stone in Canillas when I felt sick in the dirty bar, the other about a dark morning I saw Atepmoc come into light. You had said a very hurting thing to me that night, but nothing about that in the poem, it ends with a dish-washing in the grey morning. Took my bike, difficult to ride in the snow, and went to a litteraire periodical. Out of house.

Strange things happen to my Praha-story in this weeks: I cannot go on writing it. Not "Can-not" in the usual way, but because I cannot remember the years with good old Steffen any longer. I can only remember you. It is a dreadfull thing not to remember the years you had once, together with one you loved once—it means in a way that they never were there. Every time I fish for an image, one with your shows up. I am a bit horrified, must low my head again and again towards you. You, maybe roving from me.

Sweet-Anna and Strong-Jan were married last sunday. It took place in an old church from 1720 inside the Citadel of Copenhagen (a church reserved for the military, and Jan's father was a colonel)—a simple gracious church, a mixture of Lutheran clean-style (empty walls, the whiteness) and Catholic colourrichness. It was like some catholic reminders remained, among other thing a very gay, blue altar with a very golden Virgin ... no, impossible, she is removed 200 years ago in this country—it must have been the golden carpenter then.

It was a very beautifull day, snow all over, gleaming sun on the icy moats. I took my bike (freezing in shirt & stockings), I was too late, hurried through all this white silence, heard behind me another running person, but there was nobody. I glide into a bench in the front of the church, the couple-in-spee arriving just after. Anna looked like a science-fiction-Fairy-Queen in a white dress with a trembling jacket in lilac moiré, violet frecia, a Rhinestonebelt& pink nightclub-shoes. I met a danish journalist and poet at the party after, he has lived in Spain for twenty years (in Madrid and the Basque-land). I could not help talking about you, he asked: are you very happy for this person? and I said: never been so much in love, and he send me a tender glance (which I now share with you). Tender glances we all sent Anna and Jan that day. Or even more so the day after when Anna's mother, brothers, Marijke and I cleaned up the house. There was a loving mood in all the rooms, between all of us, we washed and looked marvelled at all the useless gifts, talking, drinking a little. Dreamt tonight that Larry Rivers showed up at the wedding, everybody knew him, were amazed and happy to see him. I guess he was your substitute.

How can you know that I always turn the telephonbell down to the lowest sound? I do. It rings summerly like a bee while I am making food in the evening, and Marijke spells difficult words loud and is examinating her brandnew growing nipples.

V

The Foreign Land
("The Dream Is Dreaming Me")

CHAPTER 18

Atepmoc Diary, April 1975

I stand at the window of the Bar el Montes commanding a view of the main Plaza which presents the usual fucked-up aspect—idlers, straw blown about, the church door open. I did not know what to expect: the second appearance is always different—the sauntering certainly a bluff. Through the window I watch you sail into view. You saunter across the Plaza, taking your time, you want to show me yourself advancing. Your tallness surprises, the nudeness of your ears, your hair is up. You wear a white linen shirt, a flared skirt of pale colours, you stop outside Luis Perico's bar, bend to look into a parked car, using the glass as a mirror, watchful, very calm, tall and self-possessed. The idlers stare. I open the bar door a fraction.

You see the movement, see me watching you, you make no sign. You come on, very calm, tall, unsmiling, up the ramp. I open the door just enough to let you through. You come in, tall, the pure fragrance of meliolet, the shape that sustains you, the breath that moves. The portable chess-set is on the bar counter by my gin and tonic. You ask for the same.

You had come from afar, had already spent five days in Atepmoc, were thinking of leaving, the bitch had given you a dark room; there you were with Marijke. "Do you find me masculine?" you asked as if it were a code. And I answered, "Do you find me feminine?" There it began. You had to sit for the shaking. Luis kept close watch from the kitchen, the bar was deserted. You spoke in an accent unfamiliar to me, you were several women simultaneously, come from different directions. It was the beginning.

Did I seem real to you, dearest? One day in error I'd call you by a different name, it wouldn't be your name, and all would be over between us. One day you would begin to turn away from me, I turn away from you, you leaving. I know no other life before you. Steffen Krähe drinks all evening in a strange hotel. I take you again so that my existence in you can go on. It's a dream, love is invented, we have invented it anew.

Then: the curious long kiss, your head in the clothes. Left behind: the time alone, the dead stillness, bat and lynx faces amongst the cobwebs, stirrings and gnawings in the heat of mid-afternoon, the incessant drone of flies, a small bird suspended on the wire outside. With tight nerves drawn like elastic I hear the bird fly silently away. The stirrings and gnawings continue.

Against the hill the kiln is fired, thick grey smoke gushes from the pyre, unfurling upwards, then rolling back over Atepmoc. A little girl, self-absorbed and phosphorescent, is dancing in the flames. We was shaking like mads. Gunfire sounds over the next hill. We are together at last. Time runs out in a circle.

Dream of a Liderlig Jomfru

Sometimes you had a crazy look, become the dark-complexioned tough young moll of some København gangster, the face on the expired passport. Your hands were not soft. You were a big strong Viking girl, very fierce. I held your arm. In bed that morning you had threatened to strike me. "I would like to do," you said, narrowing your lynx eyes. You could be fierce, could be gentle. You had long chorus girl's legs sheathed in black silk stockings with rose-red tops, a German fancy from *Magasin du Nord*.

It was the day you broke things. The little blue and white eggcup was the last of the Malaga set. You felt awkward and would smash things, sweeping about in an impetuous way. "I am so witchful when it is hardening up, this egg. Now I can feel it split."

You had thrown the contents of a glass of wine at me when I asked, feeble enough, Could we live in accord? I felt the cold sting as it splashed my papers, saw the wild glint in her lynx-eyes. You sat on a cushion before the fire, legs crossed, wearing only the long black stockings with the Grosz red tops, and looked daggers at me. You said: If we live together I'll have affairs *at wance*.

I buried my nose in your mossy armpit. You were my Danish meadow. You were a black mare in Little Russia. You covered your daughter in kisses. Kissed on the cheek and on the neck. "Take the child out of your mouth," Steffen said.

That carpenter Krähe, your ex-husband, Marijke's father, lives in the old street of whores, overlooking a small courtyard. He drank beer. He cooked great meals, took his daughter on long cycling trips out of town, away from people. Marijke was five then, ten now, spoke in a very superior English accent, a few words—"Good*bye*, Mr Fitzy! *Exact*ly!"

You said: "I never played little girls' games when I was young and that my unfortune." You were in many respects childish yourself, a tall awkward girl so passionate, so seeing. Silent for hours in a tree, biting your nails to the quick. You sang at the table. Old Marstrander the Socialist who played a mandolin on Labour Day, sitting on the back of a truck, said: "*La' vaer' med at synge bordet.*"

You had told me something about your people, your Pommeranian-Hungarian background—the tall Pommeranian grandmother made good soups, nipped the ends off the beans. You took after your grandmother. Standing on a cushion on a chair you sang at the top of your voice, Jesus Joy of Man's Desire. You were impatient, prone to quick rages, quick courage, sudden weeping. The parents were small-sized, frugal, careful in their spending; this made you a reckless spendthrift. You went on second weekends to their summer place in Rørvig, going on the small train to Hundested. The grandmother's maiden name was Lemm ("It means prick"). Half an hour after you were born came the small twin sister Aja, "little like an egern." Squirrel.

You had cried bitterly in the silent Atepmoc bedroom when telling me of your sister's suicide, how you had broken the news to your parents, those good people. You were the one to bring it to them. It was dark, you came stealthily to their door, "like a murderer."

Dream: What Was It Trying To Say?

It began in Denmarks Radio on Islands Brygge. You were having a conversation with the radio chiefs, Smutty Carlsen and my own boss. It wasn't in the studios or the canteen but in an office. I was in the corner typing a letter and someone uttered the name Elin. You were embarrassed and said quickly: "Yes, I had a bit of gymnastics with Elin down in Atepmoc." So I disappeared further into the corner.

171

The next picture was my house in the countryside, now quite ruined. I was there alone and the blow went all through the house, and the smell of the wet soot was very strong. I called you. I knew you were there, but you were hidden, telling something I couldn't follow, because you hid yourself constantly from me. My tongue couldn't say your name correct. I couldn't control my tongue. I called you. You didn't answer.

I was of course very unhappy because you had let me down. I knew that you had hid yourself and changed yourself into a very dangerous *something*—hardly into an animal either, but a kind of dust, if you please. Ash in a corner ready to cover me with dangerous stuff, a lethal dust. So the dream ended and I woke up with my cheeks wet of tears. And next day came your desperate letter telling of your brainstorm.

That was my dream. What was it trying to say?

Last Letter

Nørre Søgade 254
8 julio 1980

My dear,

Your letter came on the second of July, a rainy wednesday-morning, and thank you for that my love. It is mondayevening now, it is warm, I have all windows open, I am alone. Marijke is at Steffen. Sgftfujhklpaeoamn-bcbcaquapl—I don't know what to answer. I can tell you about the beatch yesterday (I was in Rørvig in this weekend the first of summer's).

The sea was lightgrey as the sand. There was a vague wind, not strong enough to create foam but enough for the sunlight to make small and jumping reflecs,—the almost unbroken seasurface is colorless, it underlines the impression of material,—moire.

As so often before when I arrive to the beatch it was nearly empty. But soon later there are several people—as usually mostly lonely gentlemen. Where are all their wifes always hiding? They are not at the beatch. I use your djelaba everywhere now, also at the beatch, I lay on it, take it on, take it off, use it as a pillow and as a tent. It is rarely too cold and

172

never too hot, it makes me feeling home everywhere, it's a kind of recidense. I am looking forward to the smell of warm sand when I go to sleep in nights.

Some strand-wanderers pass several times, especialy I noticed two, loudly talking, not exactly noisy but proud of the conversationsubject (which of the towns of Bornholm are situated southernmost). There are some people to whom everything they touch automatically become enviable to others: Think only to be them ... and to get those shoes—and those thoughts, and exactly that color of hair. They don't boast to that they are too, nearly royalistic, contented—I will say they are almost discret comparing to their contentment.

My father got some of the same, but at him the "royalistic contentment" is rather naivite. He still, in the age of 72, gets astonished that not everybody is like him. But his naivite has been wounded (or vulnerable?) during the last years from my mothers knifesharp grief. Now he marvels in an uncertain way, not in an enthusiastically. (But still he reads indifferent newspapers aloud even if you keep your forefinger on the spot in your own book.) I'm vaguely looking/listening to Margot Fonteyn telling about "The magic of the Dance" while I'm writing this. I've discovered a kind of interest for the ballet during the last years. It is new to me—like my interest of green plants in my windows. Both of its spinster-interest (spinster—what a mad word). But I'm swimming too. And write poems. It is after all youngish?

I re-read the sentence of the strand. There is something wrong. How can there be reflecs when the material was colorless? But there was. Maybe I have told about it in the wrong order?

I wear a golden chain around the waist, also at the beatch, also in the night. Try to imagine if you would like the sign. Feel a little false to wear it when you are not there. Feel half exited, half shy because of the slavelike in the sign, the supple. I am attract but know it is all a lie: I am no slavegirl.

Later.
Took my bike, went to my sister's grave (haven't been there since I last wrote to you). The flowers were full of holes because of all the rain, little snails lived in the white petals.

173

Now it rains again, the windows are open, it is difficult to find out what is the sound of the rain and what of the chestnutleaves.

(Unsigned)

Last Dream

It has been going on for some time. I am dreaming it, or it is dreaming me, for some time, particulars forgotten. A journey through some foreign country in I think winter or late autumn, a long journey now coming to an end, the terminus reached. It's late at night. The hotel is near: a low-sized place in a deserted street of dim skyline, perhaps Holland.

You are there, although I do not see you, standing beside me, *as always* (the dream wishes to convey), the Infected Charmer. A bearded fellow-traveller passes before us into the hotel, now stranger than anything I recall of Holland, become perhaps Czech. The bearded one glances back, shrugs his shoulders, in furlined overcoat reaching to below knees, as if to convey. "What, come so far, and *still* together?"

The booking into Reception is as awkward in the dream as sometimes in reality. Curious documents like large menu cards are consulted, the male receptionist bored and half-asleep. Presently he goes away with a sheaf of papers under one arm. Now a middle-aged woman with frizzled hair is crossing out lines in a heavy book, bending down, short-sighted. Without looking up she asks me in English: "And your friend—is he still breaking down doors?" She moves away before I can reply. Another male receptionist takes her place (there seem to be more receptionists than guests at this hotel), and to him I reply smoothly: "Oh no, very well-behaved these days. Breaking down doors not his style at all."

The receptionist makes no answer, still poring over documents. Discreetly you stand behind me (as sometimes in Atepmoc outside shops at night), tired out, weary of this slow booking-in. Documents are consulted and even signed by the receptionist, and papers filed away in the bureau behind. I am given nothing to sign, asked for no passport. Now other late travellers crowd around, all talking at once in a language I cannot understand. It's late, maybe early morning, they think

174

in a different language, the language of a slow-paced country with whose customs and habits I am unfamiliar. You put your arms about my neck, slowly as if sleeping, allow all your weight (56 kilo nude with amulet on) to rest on me. You seem weightless. We progress crabwise to our room, now allocated though nothing has been said nor any document signed, a large cellar-key handed over with eyes averted. We move slowly towards our room down many dim corridors. Some of the other guests are murmuring, perhaps discussing the curious custom of carrying tall girls off to bed in this manner. They seem abstracted, pace alongside us, heads down, glancing at us. It's a big hotel but somewhat shabby. The other late-night travellers leave us one by one, disappearing down long unlit corridors.

Matching the number on the heavy key I find a door. Our room is a disaster—as bad as any of the windowless Malaga rooms we frequented; it's by a toilet into which a man is already stepping, fumbling at his flies. I close the door and begin to move furniture about, you assisting in a feeble way. I cannot quite see you but you are certainly there (dream connivance), in a daze of exhaustion. There is much furniture. On the dusty lid of a closed piano a thick finger has scrawled "XI". Pulling the covers from a battered sofa I cover the piano. It will be alright, I wish to convey by this useless gesture, soon we will be together in bed. Then the loud persistent flushing of the toilet next door. On the worn carpet a four-foot snake is coiled up. It's not a real snake, just a realistic toy, a foreign joke. I throw it behind the piano, now shrouded and sinister. There, in the midst of our despair, with me moving furniture about this strange and uncomfortable room and you watching, but as if unseen, a spectre, the dream ends.

Also available in ABACUS paperback:

FICTION

ENDERBY'S DARK LADY	Anthony Burgess	£1.95 ☐
QUEEN OF SWORDS	William Kotzwinkle	£2.50 ☐
ROSE UNDER GLASS	Elizabeth Berridge	£2.95 ☐
ACROSS THE COMMON	Elizabeth Berridge	£2.75 ☐
SING ME WHO YOU ARE	Elizabeth Berridge	£2.95 ☐
THE HOUSE ON THE EMBANKMENT	Yuri Trifonov	£2.50 ☐
FOREIGN EXCHANGE	Ed. Julian Evans	£3.50 ☐
BABIES IN RHINESTONES	Sheila Mackay	£2.75 ☐

NON-FICTION

STRANGER ON THE SQUARE	Arthur and Cynthia Koestler	£2.95 ☐
NAM	Mark Baker	£2.95 ☐
PETER THE GREAT	Robert K. Massie	£5.95 ☐
IRISH JOURNAL	Heinrich Böll	£1.95 ☐
KAFKA – A BIOGRAPHY	Ronald Hayman	£3.25 ☐
TERRORISM	Walter Laqueur	£2.75 ☐
THE GREAT EVOLUTION MYSTERY	Gordon Rattray Taylor	£3.95 ☐

All Abacus books are available at your local bookshop or newsagent, or can be ordered direct from the publisher. Just tick the titles you want and fill in the form below.

Name _____

Address _____

_____

Write to Abacus Books, Cash Sales Department, P.O. Box 11, Falmouth, Cornwall TR10 9EN

Please enclose cheque or postal order to the value of the cover price plus:

UK: 55p for the first book plus 22p for the second book and 14p for each additional book ordered to a maximum charge of £1.75.

OVERSEAS: £1.00 for the first book plus 25p per copy for each additional book.

BFPO & EIRE: 55p for the first book, 22p for the second book plus 14p per copy for the next 7 books, thereafter 8p per book.

Abacus Books reserve the right to show new retail prices on covers which may differ from those previously advertised in the text or elsewhere, and to increase postal rates in accordance with the PO.